LONDON
Bites

EIGHT **STORIES**

by
Brandon Broll

To Sasha,
 With best wishes
 Brandon ✗

RIOLS
QUARTER

COPYRIGHT

Published by Riols Quarter Ltd.
85 Great Portland Street, London W1W 7LT, England
Company number: 12673832

A CIP catalogue record for this book is available
from the British Library

Paperback ISBN 978-1-913758-06-6
Ebook ISBN 978-1-913758-05-9

Cover design by More Visual Ltd.
Illustrations by Barbara Jackson

PREFACE

These eight London stories and seven London poems written between 1990-91 encapsulate another era of the city when Camden Market was edgier, Pavarotti sang in the rain in Hyde Park, and Nelson Mandela's iconic presence lit up Wembley Stadium following his release from prison in South Africa. As a fellow countryman, I had also recently arrived in London, as a political refugee refusing compulsory conscription into the white South African army. It would be four more years before apartheid was dismantled. I had trained as a scientist, published poetry and political journalism, and arrived from Cape Town in my twenties hoping to be a writer.

In London I was granted refugee status while these stories were being written, first living in the household of Denis and Esme Goldberg and then later sharing a house with their daughter Hilary. Denis was one of Mandela's co-accused at the Rivonia Trial. He had served twenty two years in prison as part of Mandela's ANC attempt to overthrow apartheid. A family connection existed between the Goldberg's and myself. I mention this because several of these London stories and poems hold a special Goldberg resonance for me as some scenes and events portrayed were experienced closely with this family. For example, the poem London Bites mentions the 'Welcome Mandela' concert at Wembley stadium. Hilary and I along with other exiled South Africans living temporarily in the Goldberg household were audience members of this groundbreaking concert which was broadcast to more than sixty countries, while backstage Denis liaised with Mandela. On that day we shared in the impending freedom celebration for South Africa that Nelson Mandela's release from prison represented and the ecstatic standing ovation when he emerged on stage urging a continuation of sanctions against the country and for people to keep pressing for the abolition of apartheid.

On a different occasion portrayed in another poem, Hilary, myself and a few close friends attended the Pavarotti in Hyde Park evening concert in the rain. While, thanks to a personal invitation from Esme, she and I sat together in the Members Enclosure at Lord's to watch the Benson and Hedges cricket Cup Final at Lord's cricket ground. Esme was an avid cricket fan and I felt honoured to accept her kind offer of a very sought-after ticket.

But perhaps the subject personifying that era in London most vividly for me, resonating the sadness of South African exiles, is the short story in this collection titled By the Vegetable Patch. I had left Esme and Denis' house in East Finchley, and at the time it was written occupied a loft room in a shared house with Hilary nearby in Crouch End.

Although London has been my home for thirty years now, the early life of an exile is acutely personal, etched with struggle, sadness, with a longing for things lost and gone, combined with attempts to gain a foothold in a newly adopted place. My place of adoption was London. Vibrant London. Capital city. Having cut my teeth as a published poet in South Africa, all poems in this volume were published in London anthologies at the time. The stories, however, my first attempts at this short fiction genre, are experimental studies triggered by my enrolment at The Writing School in London. Rightly, or wrongly, this short story format became a template into which my early experiences in 1990s London were channeled in a fictionalized form.

Brandon Broll
April 2021

DEDICATION

To the enduring memory
of the Goldberg girls:
Esme (1929-2000)
Hilary (1955-2002)

CONTENTS

LONDON BITES

I've heard it said that London bites
it was tongued by a Rastafarian from Bow,
who belly worships its fluorescent nights
"Hey man," he shrugs, "it tickles my ego".

North in Camden where a seventies revival
still yawns from tired enamelled jaws,
a long-haired palette of nuclear survival
wears boots, sunglasses, earring chainsaws.

London bites no less from within the bowel
as swallowed humanity travels underground,
down escalator throats an uttered vowel
of homelessness, others forever home-bound.

I resurface into a "Welcome Mandela" crowd
where the oval of Wembley is so open-lipped
that it roars a ragged-toothed freedom aloud,
and issues of poll tax are suddenly stripped.

Downtown an executive champs at the bit
then smiles pleasantries of a summer deal,
and the handshake of commerce is candlelit
and packaged with wine and *cordon bleu* meal.

To those lazy lawns of Parliament Hill
where wintered-skin suntans, children skitter
here where writers write in exile still,
beside the hype, the style, suburban litter.

POET'S MISSION

"Next reader to the podium please. Ladies and Gentlemen, would you give a kind welcome to our next reader…"

The Master of Ceremonies rose from his front row seat to make this announcement. No microphone was necessary. He turned obliquely towards his audience whilst at the same time was half-turned away facing the stage as the preceding performer descended the stairs. It was a manner of informal introduction that suited these small, intimate, yet sometimes boisterous poetry readings. Poetry meetings on a Sunday evening which were not without the eccentricity of London New Wave fashion, working-class heckling, raucous political satire in commentary in between the sipping of beer. The Master of Ceremonies thanked the departing poet with a nod of his head.

"Ladies and Gentlemen – our next reader is Eloise Donoghue."

Eloise's heart leapt at this mention of her name. She rose to her feet. Her hands began to shake in their nervousness, her mouth felt dry, she was breathless as she heard the applause around her.

"Excuse me..." she said, repeatedly, trying to avoid stepping on toes as she sideways shuffled along the row of seats to the aisle. For the first time tonight on an adult stage, here in Caversham Poets meeting house out in front of an expectant public audience of forty, she would perform three of her landscape poems. The best and most carefully crafted of her 'Orchid Butterfly' nature series of poems.

The experience was unprecedented. To Eloise it seemed like a life's wait for this moment. Because this instant of walking up to the stage took her all the way back to those intensely private days of her childhood scribblings of verse. When her early attempts to write and her childish literary seriousness had been praised by her foster parents as much as was her courage in coping with loneliness and despair as a young teenager trying to understand the tragic death of her biological mother when she was just a baby. From that adolescent time - to now - to this crystalline moment as she mounted the stage stairs and turned to face the audience.

It was the materialization of her London literary dream. A dream which she had taken control of with determination, with excitement, and with as much youthful courage as she could muster after her eighteenth birthday: when first Eloise had left the safety of her foster parents home on the Lincolnshire coast, to come down here to north London on this mission. A dream nurtured and grown up with her writing aspirations that with time developed a more mature resonance as she found her voice in her English landscape poetry.

Now the subtleties and word stresses, the *oeuvre* of these nature poems seemed crammed into her brain all at once. The audience had paled in the dim darkness behind strobe lights which lit three typed pages held in her hand. The lights struck her face with an intense heat.

11

At one point Eloise wasn't sure while standing and performing whether her written words were even issuing from her mouth. For years these poems had been buried unheard on these folio sheets; unheard except in her head, now at last being voiced to this receptive London audience. She concluded the 'Orchid Butterfly' epilogue and a round of applause broke out.

Eloise didn't notice the Master of Ceremonies continue with his next pronouncement. Hardly aware was she of his cordial and brief shaking of her hand. Only afterwards did she realize how sweaty her palms had become during the reading and felt embarrassed about that handshake. As she shuffled again sideways between the occupied seats to sit down from whence she had come, two more poets-from-the-floor began their own recital.

In due course the house lights were raised as the interval commenced. Eloise found herself being congratulated by the person sitting on her right who introduced himself as Edgar from Camden Lock. Edgar, apparently, was also a nature lover interested both in landscape poetry and in the east Lincolnshire coastline.

"Ever seen those toads at Theddlethorpe ?" he asked.

"No. Can't say I have."

"Have you been to Theddlethorpe dunes ?"

Eloise couldn't help out here either. Nor could she trust her concentration at this moment with the facts of his polite though rather tedious conversation. Her body still felt tense and stirred with adrenalin from being up on stage. Passively she listened as Edgar described a rare indigenous toad found in the sand and shallow pools of Theddlethorpe. Called a natterjack toad, he said brisk with authority, adding that it was distinguished by the way it runs rather than hops. Edgar was distracted in his conversation when some of the noisier members of the audience returned laughing, carrying cans of lager bought at an off-licence across the road.

People began to get seated for the second half. When the MC announced the main Caversham reader for this evening, a hush of expectation descended upon the audience as the house lights dimmed. Some people craned their necks to get a clearer view. Whereupon, in a silence of baited suspense usually reserved for poetry performers who have proven their eminence, Thomas Sickert stepped onto the stage like a heavyweight contender. His hand was heavily gloved with a book of his published work.

Eloise was struck by Thomas' face. It had a familiarity she couldn't quite put a finger on. Looking around, other faces in the audience were also galvanized to Thomas' words. His performance was unflagging - pulses of brilliance settling to a whispered rhythm which arced again and again back to a heady intensity of wordplay. She wasn't sure whether the electricity in the air was Thomas' or her reaction to him or the adrenalin still in her blood from herself having also read. It didn't matter as she listened, the gooseflesh tingling and rising on her skin.

Afterwards, while stealing a glimpse of Thomas' face at close quarters, she bought all three of his books available on sale. The dust cover reviews were as brilliant as his performance had been: "Thomas Sickert deftly combines precise and erudite pastiche with his own incisive comments..." *TBS Review*; "Anger honed into the bitterest satire and wielded by an acute intelligence" *Literary Voice*; "He creates a vivid, evocative portrait of the city of London at once raspingly harsh and continuously beautiful... his poetry blazes from the pages..." *Word Bite Magazine.*

When a group of the audience left with Thomas to take up a round of drinks at the local Kentish Town pub, Eloise hesitantly joined them and managed to secure a seat close enough to hear Thomas talk. If she could have had it her way entirely, she would somehow have attracted Thomas' attention. But Edgar from Camden Lock decided to come along too and now offered to buy Eloise a cider; half-heartedly she struck up a conversation with him whilst straining also to hear Thomas' comments from across the table. Once, Thomas' eyes caught hers - in a piercing, sustained glance - and that electricity in her veins flared once again.

It was towards the eleven o'clock last-call for drinks with Thomas blocked off from Eloise's view by the standing onlookers, that two antagonists suddenly chorused at one another, arguing aggressively some point of fact above the assembled hum of other voices. It came as quite unexpected to Eloise that one of the antagonists happened to be Thomas. Not knowing the gist of their argument she turned to see Thomas stand up solid and erect, angrily holding an empty beer glass, then he bit it. Spitting shards onto the table, Thomas' eyes watered as the drinking glass was broken by his teeth into fragments which he painfully spat out and discarded. Unable to challenge this his opponent stood smiling ironically, but then decided to walk out of the pub to whoops of decried laughter and back slapping. A minute later Thomas left the pub too.

Eloise also took her leave and quietly slipped out. She reached Thomas half-way up Torriano Avenue. She took out one of his books and tried to hand it to him opened at the title page.

"Will you autograph this for me ?"

With some annoyance Thomas stopped.

"Got a pen ?" he asked.

At close quarters under the street lighting she could see that his mouth was swollen from that dangerous glass-eating debacle back in the pub. It was bloodied and cut at one corner. Yet, to her, he had a beautiful face. When Thomas realized she had bought all three of his latest books, his tone of voice softened.

"Didn't you also read tonight ?" He spoke as though with sensitive and sore teeth.

"Yes." Eloise smiled.

When he asked her name, then confessed he recognized her east Lincolnshire accent, their eyes met again. She lowered her glance at this accent recognition. "Well if you're interested - Eloise - I'm reading again this coming Wednesday night near Clapham Junction. Here, take this complimentary ticket. I hope you can come."

*

Prodding and pushing his way out of the throng of literary people, Thomas grunted a soft: "Pah!" under his breath, as he squeezed a narrow avenue through. Some

16

patrons of the Clapham Junction club where this literary evening had been held patted him on the back. He was halted by a young girl who thrust an autograph book into his hand but he quickly (after a signing) resumed his push forward. He refused the numerous offers of *Comte de Blanzac* French champagne, so intent was Thomas to get through this panoply of literary types. He glanced backwards. Eloise was still following.

They stepped out from the Clapham hall into a clear London night. The air had an itch of cold. Thomas kept on walking, slowing down briefly for Eloise to catch up although huddled against any questions she might ask. She remained silent, simply feeling grateful that he had accepted the half-jack of Scotch she had purchased for him before the performance in appreciation of the complimentary ticket. Only when they reached the dark expanse of Clapham Common did Thomas ease his pace. He drew the whiskey bottle from his jacket pocket and swigged a mouthful. It was near Eagle Pond that they sat down on the frosty crispness of the grass.

Her mind was a mass of silent questions. While her heart felt excited by the proximity of Thomas. Not once did Eloise seriously ask herself why she was sitting in this giant moonlit park at eleven o'clock at night with the rumpled shape of a strange man beside her. This

17

moment felt right to her. She even felt a sense of spirituality being here alone with Thomas. She linked her arm with his, leaning lightly up against the tenseness of him, once turning her face to observe his darkened profile. At this proximity she could smell the tang of whiskey on his breath – a pungent odour which didn't matter. She refused an offer of whiskey herself. Time slipped by as they watched with few words the clouds scud by lit pale yellow from the London city lights. Until a church bell chimed twelve and a swan floated past in silhouette on the pond.

"We've probably missed the last tube," murmured Eloise.

Thomas moved his heavy shape against her. "I know of a place nearby that will put us up," he said.

They sat huddled together for a while longer. On the far perimeter of Clapham Common the blue light of an ambulance flashed its tiny hurried pace. It surprised Eloise, when Thomas asked her to help him to his feet, as he straightened himself upwards like a slow mechanical crane, the size of him to what had a moment ago compacted on the lawn. With his protective shape directing them along she felt a kind of ascendancy to her step: her mind flowing in a timeless bubble that she almost hoped would not break. She felt as if she had been with Thomas, with his poetic soul, always. This ascendancy to her step seemed so safe and secure no matter the eerie darkness of the tree-lined path along which they were walking.

It was then that a suspicion affected Eloise, subliminally at first as she walked arm in arm with him, that Thomas Sickert could actually be her long lost father. Her biological father. The thought seemed unbelievable. On the face of it this was possible in a number of ways, strengthening more in her mind each time she chanced to look at him. However this was not a game to play on someone. Eloise felt the need to establish the facts of this growing suspicion with much more certainty.

*

As in the park, Thomas remained introspective with his head bowed, half drunk, although now sitting on one of the two single beds in a lamp-lit B&B room into which they had booked themselves and which Eloise had paid for. Thomas leaned heavily against the headboard of the bed closest to the window. Curiously his lips moved as though he were quietly reciting rhyming couplets to himself, brooding as if lost in an inner contemplative world. Eloise decided to take a shower. To leave him alone. Afterwards she stepped out of the adjoining

19

bathroom, damp-haired and refreshed, her nakedness wrapped in a towel.

"That's better," she sighed, wringing her wet hair into a white hand towel. "Would be nice if this place supplied a bathrobe. Looks like they can afford it." She glanced up at the ornate mouldings which patterned the ceiling while sweeping the auburn mop of curls behind her shoulders. Eloise sat down beside him. "Thomas, are you alright ?"

His tired eyes were now fixed on a small pocketbook. His reading was averted when, seeing him intense like this, she put a hand on his shoulder and turned him gently to embrace her, to be enveloped in his coated bear-hug. It was a movement that inadvertently disrobed her towel which fell to the floor. When they drew apart she smiled with embarrassment into Thomas' eyes as his face scanned her youthful curves like a slow meticulous painter. He swallowed at her nakedness. He looked up at her face.

"Get covered," he said.

Thomas rose pocketing the book, then walked over to the bathroom and entered, closing the door behind himself. Eloise climbed into the second single bed. A gurgle of water began to emanate from behind the bathroom door. She thought she smelled the odour of whiskey again before she dozed off: it was a dream-like odour that lingered until she awoke to find that it had become light outside. Beyond the sash windows was the drone of morning traffic. The bathroom door was still shut.

After Eloise discovered Thomas fully clothed with his boots still on, snoring in the empty bath, she tugged him awake. She removed the bottle of whiskey he had carefully balanced on the lip of the bath. There followed an embarrassing moment when Thomas became apologetic by confessing to being sorry for having rejected her nakedness last night. Saying in all seriousness that she was the most beautiful thing he had ever seen. Eloise smiled at this childlike nature of Thomas' confession. Reassuringly she touched his shoulder as he once again apologized for having rejected that exposure of her flesh last night; of his closing the bathroom door behind it. When she admitted there had been no ulterior motive to the accidental falling of the towel, he did not seem to believe her.

They missed breakfast at their B&B due to lateness vacating the room and instead enjoyed a croissant together with strong black Colombian coffee near Clapham Junction station. In the ticket hall, Thomas became determined to do the small service of buying

Eloise a travelcard in meagre exchange for the B&B accommodation. This, she confessed, was really unnecessary. But when Thomas persisted, his determination reminded her so much of herself, of that day when she had left her foster parents in Lincolnshire with packed bags to depart on her mission to London.

"Zygmunt is Polish," said Thomas, describing one of his poet friends as Eloise glanced out of the tube train window at the uneven ropey blackness of the underground tunnel flashing past. "Last week I got word Zygmunt had been arrested for, allegedly, can you believe, stealing a woman's groceries. Artistic fools the Metropolitan police are for accusing someone with the kind of brilliant poetic talent which he possesses. They released him yesterday."

Eloise raised an eyebrow to this.

"Before I got word of it, Zygmunt had been living homeless since arriving in London from Warsaw. Imagine a poet as remarkable as him coming to London to stay in that rat-infested cardboard city of boxes under Waterloo Bridge. He needs my help. Our train will soon be passing through Waterloo."

Eloise listened without need to reply. It was sufficient just to be holding onto Thomas' arm.

"Would you care to meet the Polish Zygmunt ? He's a damned fine poet, Eloise."

"Thanks - but not today - I must be heading off home. Let's meet next Sunday at Caversham Performance House again ? There is something important I must tell you then."

Thomas glanced inquisitively at her. After pausing, he rummaged in his tweed jacket pocket to extract a scrap of paper. "Aye, do you know Eloise... there is something I need to tell you too." He began to write down in a flourish of pencil what appeared to be verse. Briefly their eyes met in acknowledge-ment. When Waterloo station approached Thomas pressed the scrap of paper into her hand, stooped to kiss her cheek, then was gone with the clash of train doors.

Your youth, Eloise
And butterfly trust

I can't bring myself
To crumple your wings

The powder of you
Easily stamped underfoot

I must protect it
Though I don't know why ?

Of course, secretly, Eloise knew why. She suspected why Thomas felt a mysterious need to protect her, although he was as yet unaware of the circumstance of their meeting – in truth without a clue - that he may be her father. Except now she felt convinced. All the facts fitted into place. And looking back with hindsight she realized why she had sensed that strong link to him, felt strangely light-headed in his presence and tantalized when first experiencing Thomas' electric performance on-stage. From the time when her foster parents had taken her aside on her eighteenth birthday and informed her that her father was still alive, she had wondered with awe about this possibility.

After buying his poetry books on that first night, she had scoured the biographical pages to establish where and when he was born. After recognizing the physical features of him on stage, his eyes, his bearing, his poetic sensitivity, which seemed so oddly familiar. Even the odd circumstances around her birth - information which she had received from her foster parents - matched the anonymous discussions she had had with Thomas this morning as to his situation when her true mother had been abandoned by him when Eloise was a baby.

And now strangely, after spending a night together in a south London B&B, she felt she could forgive him.

Easily forgive him. After all these years he was still unable to look after himself properly. His drinking problem remained unquelled. But talented poets, she knew, like other artists and performers are often afflicted in this way. In this respect her foster parents had been a godsend in having raised her better than ever he could have done. On the sudden death of Eloise's mother, Thomas had suffered a bout of mental illness, ending up homeless for years and at that time losing custody of her.

Yes, she thought, I forgive him. I too am a performance poet now - perhaps he will let me care for him. In her deep contemplation of Thomas, Eloise felt self-contained no matter all of the underground passengers also travelling in this tube compartment. Cut off from the rest of them as she slowly re-read his poem on the precious scrap of paper he had given her, the train carrying her northwards into the London suburbs: worming its way underground, distancing further and further from Waterloo.

CLAY REMOULDING

The thud of a blackboard duster banged by hand on an old tin plant-pot, in quick, loud, repeated succession, resounded hardly at all above the voices in the classroom. To this there was little response beyond a few turned and bemused faces. The adult students had clustered into three fragmented groups at the far windows. Now raising an outstretched arm to them, the poetry tutor, duster still in hand, cleared his throat to speak.

"*Attention, s'il vous plait.* Your attention, please !"

It took some minutes before the adult conversation hushed to a consensus of silence.

"If you'd all be so kind as to take your seats."

The poetry tutor extracted a wad of papers from a thick, well-thumbed and weather-beaten cardboard folder which he had placed on his desk at the front of the class.

"Here," he said, "divide these photocopies amongst yourselves. Tonight we will be analyzing an ode by Pablo Neruda, the great Chilean poet, winner of the Nobel Prize for literature in 1971, before we get on to discuss your own writing." A few student faces showed surprise that tonight they would be studying a South American poet but on the whole the interest of the group was aroused.

Caiona felt equally pleased. Not least that this evening they were learning about Neruda, but just by being present here in the poetry class, sitting second row from the front meant an entirely different environment from home. When she had chosen these poetry evening classes on Mondays, Caiona had made the decision on the spur of the moment like an addict desperate for a fix from the mundane: intolerably heavy-headed and almost desperate for a lightness of being. Feeling like a wife who had been forgotten, she was touched with a desperation to escape and free her mind from the domestic drudgery of home.

Over the next twelve weeks of Mondays she had hired a child-minder without even asking Richard's consent, deciding to attend these night-classes alone at the nearby Camden Institute. At a time of evening when Richard was still happily shackled to his office work.

At the end of the class tonight with each participant drained from their solo poetry performances, it was customary for members of the group (including their French tutor) to relax with a drink.

"Partake of a pint," the tutor joked in his broad French accent. The local 'Spud and Lettuce' pub was a minute's walk down from the Camden Institute.

"Coming with us, Caiona ?"

She glanced at Ninon's expectant and companionable face, hesitating at a reply. "I'm afraid I can't make it. Not tonight..." Caiona said, smiling in a measure to hide her uncertainty. There seemed no time for such a luxury. Richard would soon be returning home from the office. Caiona's eyes followed the arched perspective of the darkened corridor through which they were walking toward its entrance. "Maybe next week will be easier on my time."

Ninon shrugged her shoulders in response, rotated a hand palm up in disappointment. Ever since joining the poetry class Caiona had reacted this way, which, of course, fair enough Ninon felt, was her prerogative. It was her choice if she preferred to be unsociable. But that wasn't what seemed odd to Ninon. It was more the gaunt ambivalence on Caiona's face: like she were carrying with her a shadow of resentment when the simple question to "partake of a pint" was contemplated. As if she really wanted to go along with the group but was refusing against her will.

"Is there anything wrong, Caiona ?"

She did not answer this question.

"Or perhaps I shouldn't pry," said Ninon. "I am sorry."

Caiona half-smiled in recognition of this apology. "Look, thanks for offering but I ought to be heading off home." Caiona veered down another corridor of the Institute, her heels echoing a staccato click on the stone floor.

"Wait !"

Ninon reached her.

"Forgive me, I shouldn't have pried into your affairs... Really, I apologise for being so tactless."

Caiona eased visibly at this courtesy.

"C'mon, how about it," prompted Ninon. "Just one tiny little beer ? It's impossible to talk to you personally during class and, well, I feel an affinity towards you, Caiona." She struck a moment of sustained eye-contact. "Can't we try to be friends ?"

Caiona surveyed the stonework mosaic of the floor. The arched Victorian corridor was empty now and getting colder, which made Ninon's offer of warmth and friendship seem inviting in this stark red brick passage. Equally so, Ninon saying that she sensed an affinity towards Caiona felt in strange contrast to Caiona's own desire to escape: exactly that runaway urge from home which had attracted her here to these poetry evening classes in the first place, was driving her irrationally away down this corridor back to Richard.

"I don't understand," said Caiona. "You say you feel an affinity. But we're such opposite people."

"Hah !" Ninon snuffled. "C'mon, all I'm asking is you accompany us for a pint. No psychoanalysis involved."

"One drink then," Caiona finally conceded.

The 'Spud and Lettuce' pub was a'buzz with locals. Some of the poetry class students had found seats in an alcove, dark oak-beams low over their heads, while others had huddled into an adjoining group. Ninon threw a glance in their direction.

30

"Not a twopenny bit of space with them," she said. "What do you want to drink, Caiona ?"

"Newcastle brown, please."

"Mmmm… I'll join you in that."

In this pub environment Ninon seemed completely at home leaning sideways with an elbow on the counter. She hailed: "Two Newcastle brown ales" above the beat of a James Brown classic being played. "Shall we perch ourselves over there?" Ninon said, pointing at two bar stools.

In the half-hour which followed Caiona was struck by the gaping chasm of personality difference that seemed to separate her from Ninon. She realized that a massive difference lay in their everyday values to life. No matter Ninon's honest attempts to draw and tie together conclusions about the similarities they shared: of them both being expatriates in London, after Ninon recognized Caiona's southern Irish accent and then spoke of her own family link with France. This similarity meant nothing to Caiona. What Caiona couldn't shake off, what she found quite irreconcilable, was the fact that Ninon remained a single woman out of choice: neither was she in a stable relationship, nor was she a mother. Who besides that was proud of it. Ninon, she learned, was an *avante garde* fighter for Women's Rights and a self-proclaimed feminist poet. Neither did Caiona care about their ages being the same. These other vast differences between them she just couldn't shake off: the fact that she, herself, was a married mother-of-two. In this aspect of their lives lay a chasm of difference - Ninon's independence and her powerful feminist assertiveness - was at the moment quite undigestable.

It was in the talk of retro fashion that Caiona grasped exactly the extent of this freedom for which Ninon stood. Ninon looked so vibrant and young and clear-eyed sitting there with her short spiked hair, her slimness - almost too thin - was accentuated by a black body-outfit and the angular hardness of her pale features. She listened as Ninon talked animatedly with expressive hands about a black leather boutique on the King's Road in Chelsea. That she owned it and was planning to open another boutique in north London in the vicinity of Hampstead.

In this topic of fashion, Ninon's conversation had finally struck a common point of interest they both could share. As they talked this pub atmosphere was becoming relaxing to Caiona. The other members of the poetry class also seemed to be enjoying themselves. And before Caiona knew it, caught dreamily, slightly drunkenly off guard, she found herself agreeing, nodding in the affirmative to this very persuasive classmate of hers.

"All right Ninon. But phone me first," Caiona replied.

This new Hampstead boutique of Ninon's was close enough to Caiona's East Finchley home, so that why, Ninon explained, why shouldn't they try to meet up at a lunchtime when she was around working in the vicinity ? As exciting and interesting as discovering a new friend seemed to Caiona, certain issues which Ninon was raising, especially the values of independence for which she stood, made Caiona feel nervous.

"First phone me to check," Caiona reiterated with added hesitation. "I really prefer to confirm any meeting we may have, closer to the day."

*

In her own inimitable style, sitting offbeat in a sunflower-yellow sundress with inky black hair, Ninon sipped at her iced-tea. She wore three silver sleeper earrings in one ear upon which dangled tiny silver fish. Removing the dark sun-glasses from against her pale features, she admired the amber coloured vase positioned like an oriental sculpture on the table.

"You know Caiona you're an accomplished artist," she said, turning the vase slowly by its thin stem in a delicate twirl, noticing Caiona's initials imprinted on the side of the base. "It's true - I do agree with that Earl's Court catalogue - your pottery does have a kind of Japanese elegance."

"Why thanks."

"Are you still an active potter ?"

"Hah..." Caiona averted her eyes. Her snigger was one of self-derision. "That catalogue is ten years old at the least. I haven't worked clay or ceramics in absolute ages. I can't even remember exactly how I glazed that particular piece."

Ninon was examining the vase at eye-level.

"But look at your talent..."

Instead, Caiona looked out of the nearby sash window into the small enclosed garden where a ginger cat was crossing the lawn, and put a finger to her mouth biting at the varnished nail.

"God, it must really be that long ago !" she said in disbelief. "Yes, I do remember now when it was. I had just turned twenty four years old when I fired that vase." Her eyes continued to follow the cat as it leapt up onto a wooden fence. While observing the cat's balanced movements she remarked casually: "Too busy these days being a mother – I guess."

Ninon turned to a cabinet beside the tea table where they were sitting. Inside the cabinet were dinner plates, each with a colourful hand-painted *motif* of iris flowers.

"And those ? Are they also yours ?"

Caiona shrugged her shoulders feeling faintly embarrassed at all this attention which was being heaped on her old pottery work. Work the significance of which she had long forgotten after having become a mother. "Maybe someday I'll get back into it."

"But they're exquisite pieces !"

"Gosh." Caiona smiled. "I haven't received appreciation like this in years."

Ninon's eyes remained serious and intense, and her bearing on the subject was one of determined exposure. "Well while I'm heaping praise on you, I may as well say that your poem - 'Kites on Hampstead Heath' - which you read to us so modestly last Monday night at the Camden Institute deserved every bit of the ovation it received. I loved it."

After lunch, once Ninon had left for work at her new leather boutique, Caiona found herself once again alone in the house but mesmerised by that near tidal wave of praise, uplifted by the enthusiasm which Ninon had displayed like some forgotten feeling of teenage seduction. So overwhelmed was she by these possibilities that she went to retrieve her file of poetry workshop scribblings to re-admire that poem which, in truth, had aroused quite a good ovation at the Camden night class.

But still this effusion regarding her talents seemed almost incomprehensible to Caiona. True, she could feel her heart flutter with the self-indulgence of thinking about these words of praise. Yet behind this excitement which she was suspicious of - behind Ninon's lunchtime visit - there also lurked a dark undertone. As if she, Caiona, the supposed talented artist and the once aspiring potter had allowed her talents and her once serious career aspirations to be completely forgotten here at home by her own family. Instead of having followed these dreams long ago, in the eye of her family now she was solely seen as a mother who, even at her young age, found herself already having to reminisce about her talents. Why didn't Richard show her this kind of appreciation? Caiona steadied her nerves. Tried to take a hold of her rising emotions. It felt a whole lot easier to dismiss Ninon's effusive comments as just being over the top: after all, she thought, I'm not some kind of budding genius ! I'm merely a housewife with an artistic gift. Happy enough as a housewife for goodness sake.

"Artistic expression, Caiona, is yours to PROTECT," Ninon continued passionately a week later. "It's unnecessary to share this expression of ourselves with men. After all these are OUR talents - yours and mine." As their friendship progressed along these lines so a militant feminism which was a part of Ninon's confidence seeped to undermine, subtly, yet with definite purpose, Caiona's calm.

"Is anything bothering you ?" asked Richard late one evening after work had kept him at the office.

Caiona shrugged off the question which to her had developed an undertone. Instead she entered the kitchen to heat up Richard's dinner and sort out the children's school lunches. Those familiar silences which she experienced with such heaviness, sometimes even dread during the day, when the family were up and gone, were beginning to seep into these long family evenings: it led to a personal resentment when Richard and the children were wrapped up in themselves at home. And whatever the family's plans had been to redecorate the house, Richard's work pre-occupation to earn money towards this end had also begun to infuriate her. He seemed so fulfilled in his work, so bloody-minded about the money-earning process of it, that she didn't notice an element of real concern in Richard's voice and dismissed his question - his honest appeal - as if it were a joke. Secretly she had even begun to question her feelings about the success of their marriage. A marriage not yet outwardly discussed with Ninon, but which their lunchtime conversations had begun to hedge around with enough suspicion to force her awake one night.

Beside her Richard lay there baby-faced in sleep. He was peaceful. Silent. Looking at him, Caiona cursed inwardly his work preoccupation, his late homecomings from the office always with new business deals, while at the same time thinking with admiration about Ninon's outgoing drive and aggression for life. What have I become, she wondered half-propped up in bed ? The soft *pate'* inbetween each of their lives ! This pent-up anger at herself, at her lost independence (and why, she thought, can't I assert myself) forced Caiona at this late hour out of bed. In the kitchen she brewed herself a mug of Colombian coffee – choosing to take it strong and black. After a few mouthfuls, she dialled Ninon.

"Are you awake..." Caiona's tone sounded urgent and edgy into the telephone. "Can we meet tomorrow at lunchtime ? Please, I need to talk."

"What's the time ?" Ninon groaned with tiredness. "Do you realize that it's 3 o'clock on a weekday morning. Caiona, are you alright ?"

"No !" said Caiona and put down the phone.

The following day in a mood of apprehension, feeling more than a tinge of alarm, Ninon arrived early for their lunch in East Finchley.

"It's my marriage," Caiona began with a degree of caution in her voice. Nervously she bit at the fingernail of her little finger. "Every time you and I discuss art or fashion or pottery, never mind our poetry, when we dream our dreams, I feel completely trapped as a housewife. Your talk excites me - yes – but then afterwards I'm left frustrated and alone, waiting here for the kids or Richard, you rushing off looking so driven and free."

"Sounds like your marriage is choking you ?"

"I don't know, Ninon. I'm scared."

Not usually prone to physical affection, Ninon suddenly took Caiona's hand in hers. "What I see," she confessed in a tone as firm as steel, "is a woman afraid of expressing herself. Afraid of where your talents might lead you..."

"But I've got little time for talents."

"Rubbish !" Ninon's voice was resentful, her unwavering eye-contact caused Caiona to look down. "Is Richard really worth all this frustration ? Worth the long dragging periods of waiting... I'm asking this because I

39

care that you feel guilty simply going to a pub. That on sleepless nights you phone me in the early hours of the morning in an unhappy state to complain about your repressed talents while Richard continues quite happily to work late at the office."

Caiona agreed to Ninon's suggestion of a period of thought to consider her priorities, free of counsel from family members: Richard would probably only complicate and dominate her wishes if he knew what she was thinking at this stage. So she began long afternoon walks on Hampstead Heath. Which weren't easy walks at all. Caiona came down hard upon herself. How much of my talent have I wasted over these years of marriage, she interrogated herself. And for what ? Waiting for Richard ? On the spur of an existential moment she went off to buy herself an offbeat autumn outfit which she knew Ninon would adore, but Richard probably wouldn't. One day returning home from the Heath she burst uncontrollably into tears seeing her elegant self-inscribed pottery and ceramic plates in the cabinet displayed like so many relics of a past life. In bed, she spurned Richard's advances.

Caiona's desperation reached a pitch one evening driving back from her Monday poetry workshop. Returning home from the Camden Institute she chose to avoid her usual route down the Bishops Avenue, north London's millionaire row, because the colonnaded facades of homes implied so strongly in her mind family success, togetherness in marriage, riches in life. While her mood on this detour of driving down the side streets was one of dread, of wasted opportunities ! When she arrived on this particular evening on the day before her thirty fifth birthday, again Richard wasn't at home…

*

A gentle tugging of the blanket the following morning woke Caiona and she was about to turn her back on her husband as she had repeatedly done for weeks now, when she realized that the playful tugging movement was originating from children's hands.

"Happy Birthday, Mum !" they giggled.

Both her daughter and younger son were standing beside the bed with smiles of mischief on their cleanly washed faces. When Richard entered the bedroom with a birthday breakfast tray, a sing-along ensued and Caiona received birthday cards and hand-made children's gifts. Afterwards, the children departed with Richard in order to be driven to school. Before he left Richard promised her that tonight there would be a special family celebration dinner out at their favourite restaurant.

Of this promise she felt impassive. Quite unmoved by the thought of Richard probably taking time off work today to hunt for her birthday present. She retrieved her workshop file of poetry from the writing desk and climbed back into bed. Ninon is absolutely right about the marriage compromises I've made ! Even more than ever now there seemed grounds for Ninon's hardened cynicism towards men, she thought. Damn it, she cursed to herself whilst staring into the file of scribbled poetry – her attempts at creative writing - how could I have so squandered my independence ?

Half an hour later the doorbell rang. Through net curtains Richard's car could be identified pulling up into their driveway behind a workman's van which had already parked. Caiona rushed into the bathroom to shower and dress herself. When she re-emerged wearing body-fit black leggings and an offbeat tan and grey sweat shirt that she had recently purchased on Portobello Road as a birthday gift to herself, not yet worn until now, the workman's van outside seemed to have departed and Richard was waiting in the sitting room. This scene of him innocent and nonchalant on the sofa raised her hackles.

"What are you doing away from work ?"

"I like that new outfit you're wearing," Richard said offering a smile.   She ignored this comment.

"Well why are you home ?"

He stood up. "Come with me. I have something to show you..." Again he smiled, mysteriously this time, then took her hand.

"Don't touch me !" Caiona drew away.

"Cai, what's wrong ? It's your birthday."

Finally it was these last words that did it. The lovey-dovey spooning nickname "Cai", the innocent "what's wrong", the fact of her "birthday", and now he had decided to make up some time to be with her - all raced to converge on Caiona's bottled state of mind and of Richard's total ignorance of it. She felt herself explode in a fury of counter attack. And with every accusation she cast angrily at him, so Richard's face whitened. Until she had shouted herself hoarse, was tear-soaked, and was prevented from further pounding on his arms and chest when his hands gripped around her wrists. What struck Caiona then was Richard's tone of voice. He spoke with an odd kind of hurt which she had never heard him utter before.

"If nothing else, let me give you this," Richard's voice was almost inaudible. The finality of her anger had been that great. He released her wrists. She couldn't exactly determine his state of mind when he trod round-shouldered out of the sitting room, glancing once back at her. As Caiona followed she stopped, blinking tears away and to gain balance. Richard passed through the garage door into the interior of the garage which had a musty smell and was dark. Unsure of his motives, she called out his name.

"I'm not sure whether it's over between us," Richard replied, his voice hollow and plaintive as she stepped over the threshold into the darkness of the garage. "But please," he said with a stutter, "do our family at least the favour of having a look at this."

He switched on the garage lights. Caiona's eyes focused down onto a squarish object positioned waist-high on the floor, covered in a chequered blanket.

"What is it ?" Her tone remained abrupt.

Richard circled the contraption. His shoulders remained stooped as if all the enthusiasm he had first shown in the sitting room was sucked from him like marrow into a surgeon's syringe. Even his unveiling of the potters kiln was devoid of animation, and neither did he care to look at her reaction when he pulled off the blanket. Simply he stared at the kiln as a convict stares at a convicting judge.

Caiona's mouth dropped open. "I don't believe it. How did you know ? Hah..." she put a hand to her mouth in astonishment, then carelessly wiped her nose on her sleeve.

For a time they were both silent. Far apart. Standing before the potter's kiln. After a while Caiona walked up to the look on Richard's face. An expression she still couldn't understand or quite believe.

"How did you know ?"

"I..." Richard spoke deeply injured. "We've..." Her spine tingled at his apparent hurt. "We've had to watch the agony you've been putting yourself through lately," said Richard. "And we've been suffering too: both the children and myself, without you prepared to speak to me about it, withdrawing each day more and more into yourself. Twice I came home to find your ceramic plates removed to places where you were examining them. So..." he gestured at the kiln.

Caiona took both of his hands. But he looked away.

"So it's time," he continued. "The children and I discussed it amongst ourselves, that we would get you properly organised with what you once liked to do. Use the garage as a pottery workshop if you like..."

These words struck Caiona with a numbness. She thought of Ninon. She wanted Ninon to be here at this moment. To have witnessed this. Did any of the men in Ninon's world also possess a heart ? Or had Ninon ever dared to look ? Caiona placed her arms around her husband and sighed against him, feeling the tautness of his hurt as he, too, held her. Silently she thought against his shoulder: so close, my God, that was so close. Realizing just then how terrifyingly close she had come to almost declaring their marriage at an end.

"I think I may be alright Richard," she said, pulling away and seeing the image of herself reflected in his eyes.

LONDON LEAF CASCADE

A ninety-one day undressing,
a striptease floor show
on outside pavements;
three months
of cooling, peeling,
the tube train poster
makes autumn official: 91 days.

From Heathrow to Crouch Hill
is a slow ushering in -
uncapping, disrobing,
as night
waterfalls drizzle,
and we begin the breezy shiver.

While a horse-chestnut drops
its brown conker bombs
at squirrels -
who defuse, bury them
beneath
soggy earthworm soil,
there's sweetening leaf odours.

To Barnet, Bromley, to Ewell
where an overcast broken
blue of sky pales,
and our sun
arcs southwards -
to the warm Capricorn Tropics.

Leaving us mustard and ochre
in rattle of foliage,
a striptease wind
that flays, moults,
uncovers
the horizon in
a plunging neckline of trees.

In twig crunch of nightwalk
I stroll Shepherd's Hill,
past trucks frictioning
an icy tarmac,
then a fox darts
across, away, fast as summer
behind a wind eddy of leaves.

THE APRIL LICENSE

As they drove, Mr Vodjani, not native to England, initially here as a political refugee, sat in a silence of pleasant contemplation. From the passenger seat he glanced out at the passing urban scenery and brightening climate of the sky. He hated the formality of being labelled driving instructor number 24 by his North London driving school. A formality which he considered counterproductive when trying to gain the confidence of his driving students. So, at the earliest opportunity, he removed his numbered instructor's badge when away from the school and insisted that his students call him Mr Vodjani.

Today, happily, Mr Vodjani noticed in the criss-cross of streets that the colours of spring had begun to usher in. It was that time of year of the vernal equinox when British clocks are brought forward to accommodate the increasing daylight on the brink of April, time of year in the metropolis when its vastness of terraced housing, tree-lined avenues and open parks, entertains the extraordinary greening of nature.

Mr Vodjani enjoyed nature. And this morning he noticed how sudden the spring change had erupted in the naked webs of branches that were the pavement trees. On tips of these branches was a green sprouting profusion of buds, green fingertips of buds that made the local woods and parklands nearby no longer assume a winter starkness. In some places on the ground in clusters, as they drove by, there was the early flowering of blue-bells. While on traffic islands there were tussocks of daffodils which were thick and sprouting profusely, and on lawns the crocuses had come into flower in a variety of shades of white, mauve and pink.

Inwardly it cheered him to see this March to April spring transformation. The days were becoming noticeably warmer, in which the human population outside as busy as ever in London was unshelling itself from the previous winter starkness. The winter fashion of coats and scarves was definitely on the wane among pedestrians as more and more cyclists had begun to take to the roads. Indeed today the pedestrians outside seemed in quite a sunny mood standing on pavements or smiling while crossing the road or waiting for the traffic lights to change.

Mr Vodjani fingered his collar with forefinger and thumb, loosening the half-Windsor knot of his tie. In this – his eighth driving lesson with Lailla Khalvati - he now felt he should relax his close instruction of her and simply let her get on with it, knowing that by now she ought to have developed her own driving style. He made this decision with a distracted glance at the greening scenery outside before, suddenly, the car lurched forward under Lailla's control, the engine bursting into a shrill rising whine. Mr Vodjani tensed at the quickly gathering forward momentum. As the speed of the car increased further, he sat bolt upright.

"Hey, go easy !" he commanded.

In a matter of moments the vehicle was careering at breakneck speed, an illegal speed, bearing down rapidly towards a pedestrian who was inching their path across the road a hundred paces away.

"Easy," Mr Vodjani repeated. "Stay calm now Lailla. Take control. Remember what I've taught you."

But Lailla's accelerator foot remained fixed in the down position.

"Not that pedal... the other pedal. Move to the brake, apply the brake !"

Seeing still no reaction from her foot which was thrust as if frozen to the floor, the pedestrian looming larger and larger in the windscreen, Mr Vodjani, being the professional that he was, had little choice but to take evasive action. Not a moment too soon he engaged his set of controls by switching transmission, then spun the car wheel at an angle so as to swerve over the zebra crossing causing the elderly pedestrian to stagger untouched in the car's passing wind vortex.

"Shiver me..." Mr Vodjani exhaled when he had brought the car to a halt at the next curb. For some minutes they sat in a shocked silence together, his heart pounding furiously in his ears. At last he turned to her.

"Lailla, what in blazes went wrong over there ?"

"I'm not sure," her voice quavered.

"But you know that you must slow down for pedestrians where zig-zags lead to a zebra crossing..."

She nodded blankly.

"Well what happened ?"

"My foot just froze on the accelerator."

He stared at her, then screwed up his eyes to the morning light. "C'mon you've got to be joking. Are you're winding me up ? Your foot froze on the accelerator, after eight driving lessons ?"

"No I mean it."

"Look, out here on the road we're dealing with people's lives, Lailla. A car is a dangerous weapon !"

"I know... I'm sorry !" With unsteady hands she covered her face as her voice broke with the shock and emotion of it, and she began to cry. "I'm giving up learning to drive," she said sobbing through her fingers. Reaching for a tissue from her shoulder-bag on the back seat, a cluster of silver bangles tinkled with the shaking of her wrist.

Mr Vodjani sat back. "Now that's a bit extreme." His voice softened as he looked at her. "Come on Lailla, we've got this far already. There are just four more lessons to go and you will be ready. Try concentrating on what I've taught you. Try to apply the practical things we've spoken about to the road. And try to relax more.

Really, the rules of the road are very straightforward, very logical, if you perhaps review them one more time."

"No. I've tried enough," Lailla cried adamantly, shaking her head in frustration, her eyes brimming with an anger which he had never witnessed before. She stared with a seriousness out of the windscreen, her jaw-line jutting and strengthening in its purpose. "The truth of the matter is: I'm nervous driving ALONE with you."

Mr Vodjani was taken aback. Pausing awhile at this harsh statement, he ran his fingers over his moustache, smoothing and stroking the bristles with a circular movement. Then after some thought he began a fervent search for his driving instructor's identity badge in the dashboard compartment. He located it under a pile of crumpled documents, retrieved it, and held it out to her. "This is my instructors ID," he said. "I come recommended by the British School of Motoring. You can trust me, Lailla."

Frowning at him she bit at her lip. On seeing his outstretched identity badge her expression changed to one of mild embarrassment. "No, it's not that. Not that exactly," she hesitated, gaining more time for thought than seemed to warrant. "Maybe if we talked... Maybe if we broke those deep silences we seem to have while I'm driving, maybe I'd feel more at ease."

He shrugged his shoulders. "Is that what you want ? Alright, I'm happy if that's what it takes."

Lailla seemed obviously relieved as she reclined her head onto the head-rest which gave her a better view of herself in the rearview mirror. She wiped at her smudged eyeliner with the already used tissue, then retrieved another from her bag. When she was done she pushed her hair from her face and turned to look him directly in the eye. "Then tell me, Mr Vodjani, do you have an opinion about marriage engagements ?"

*

This career of driving instructor which Mr Vodjani had once envisaged for himself to be a profession with few complications had in retrospect turned out to be neither so simple nor straightforward. As arduous as his training had been to become a British driving instructor, it had merely prepared him for instructing clients who lacked the necessary driving skills and confidence in the road, like Lailla, before now.

However, Mr Vodjani found himself at this moment balking at the rather odd circumstance in which Lailla had asked this personal kind of question. A question out of the blue, which, if he dared answer, broke his own rule of not becoming too familiar with any of his clients. Had a friend asked him this question he would not have hesitated to discuss the subject of marriage engagements.

What aroused his suspicions also was his numerous past experiences of odd clients. In Brixton some of the jokers – his clients - had been more intent on car crime than a car license. While the highbrow Mayfair or Sloane set quite openly confessed to him that his modest car just wasn't the thing to be taught in. Certain other Totteridge women fluttered and batted their eyelashes at him with low glances and invitations to high tea. Or what about last Wednesday evening when Tim Ballad had turned up for his driving lesson so inebriated after a vodka-tasting birthday party that for half an hour he lay in an alcoholic stupor on the backseat ?

Mr Vodjani contemplated the meaning of Lailla's words while slipping his ID card into his breast pocket. In the past he usually felt he had been right to hesitate passing off an odd personal question asked of him. But this time he found it equally difficult to conclude that Lailla was another of those jellow-jacket crackpot customers. As he glanced sideways she had composed herself with hands placed correctly on the steering wheel. On her finger was an engagement ring.

"When you're ready," he commanded with authority, "reverse here into Nelson Mandela Close, then take a left turn to pass over the North Circular into Southgate."

Lailla nodded. She drove off with caution. He became intrigued as to why this attractive woman sitting here beside him with the surname Khalvati, obviously quite secure in her Iranian youthfulness, dark brown eyes and a sparkling smile, why in her position of 'engagement' security should she be so insecure ? As to voice it to a stranger instructing her in driving lessons ? She glanced at him sideways.

"You must think I'm crazy," Lailla said.

"I'm not judging you."

Unknown to her Mr Vodjani was himself still single and he believed in making lawful the right relationship. This was as much part of his culture as it was Lailla's notwithstanding the fashion of London's co-habitees. But engagements ? Neither was that particularly unusual considering their Iranian backgrounds. Even though most English-born couples in 1990s London co-habited without any ties, many casting away the formalities of marriage altogether.

"It's a personal preference, I suppose, to get engaged," said Mr Vodjani. "Depending on your culture..."

Lailla drove steady and confident. At their next lesson Lailla strapped herself into the car, immediately unlocking the steering as she turned the ignition. "I've waited a whole week for this," she said with enthusiasm. Typically, when starting her previous lessons, she began with some trepidation: adjusting the driver's seat in silence, rearview mirror double-checks, testing the indicators in an overkill fashion. Now with a minimum of nervous fuss they were on their way.

Mr Vodjani raised an eyebrow to this. The profile of her face was visible in his dashboard mirror by which he normally monitored the driver's response to his commands. Lailla's complexion was olive-skinned with thick almond-coloured hair, of Middle Eastern extraction like he was, and today she looked radiant. During their previous driving lessons he had established that culture-wise, although from a conservative background, Lailla was a modern London woman. Articulate by English standards. Well-travelled. Streetwise. She even joked how ridiculous it sometimes felt wearing an engagement ring. Though she never once mentioned her fiance.

An easy level of conversation continued, a light and easy formality that sometimes strikes up between a driving instructor and their student. They spoke of London happenings: an exhibition opening at the Tate gallery; the

Bolshoi and Royal ballet seasons; Hyde Park events; they even once discussed Middle Eastern politics. It was a level of easy and enjoyable conversation that continued until Mr Vodjani chanced, one lesson, upon Lailla gazing at him through his instructor's side-mirror. Her gaze happened at a yield sign while the car was stationary: her eye contact, sustained for a moment longer than suspicion would allow, left him puzzled. It left him light-headed. Lailla dismissed this provocative glance without a word.

Neither was this provocation solved when on both her eleventh and then final lesson Lailla arrived no longer wearing her engagement ring ! Mr Vodjani decided to be diplomatic. As usual remain tactful. He would not pry. Nothing was mentioned about it. He waited for her to broach the subject, yet as diffident as she was to discuss herself or the disappearance of the engagement ring, so Lailla's interest remained eager in trying to understand his viewpoints about marriage.

This Mr Vodjani found maddening. Whether it was some game of feminine mystique or merely her final burst of driver's concentration, the last ten minutes of the final lesson of their advanced instruction were completed in the old cold silence. Though now he had little doubt that Lailla would pass her driving test.

*

The thing which infuriated and nagged at Mr Vodjani in the workdays that followed, as he resumed his routine of signing on new learner drivers and completing the advanced instruction of others, was this enigma as to why Lailla Khalvati aroused in him the feelings that she did. At the completion of her driving course he had felt used. Felt as if he were left balancing in air. Equally he believed his honesty had been betrayed. Having voiced his heart on personal matters, on his lifestyle as a single man to the extent sometimes of almost being interrogated by all her probing questions, in the end she hadn't the courtesy even to explain that sudden absence of her engagement ring. He doubted that she had on the spur of a moment become 'disengaged' because her calmness in driving and her ability to concentrate on the road had improved markedly with the new conversation they had struck up. It was a week later when he heard again from Lailla.

"I've cracked it," she shouted ecstatically into his mobile phone. "I passed my driving test !"

With an air of detachment Mr Vodjani congratulated her. Indeed it was pleasing to hear of her success as it reflected on his successful training of her. Nonetheless, his words remained cool and had a sharp edge when he wished her a safe driving future ahead.

"Let's go out and celebrate. I want to treat you to a meal ?"

"Lailla, that isn't necessary."

She paused at the distancing in his voice. Her euphoria, earnest as a teenager, sobered at his icy tone and his apparent abruptness.

"Please Mr Vodjani. Allow me, I owe you this."

So it was that that evening he found himself quite half-heartedly *en route* to a restaurant, to a converted river barge moored on the southbank of the Thames where they were to meet. While commuting, Mr Vodjani sat silently engulfed in a mood of ambivalence wondering why on earth he had agreed to this dinner in the first place. Haven't I done enough for her ? She passed her driving test: what more does she want ! When she had phoned, it was true though, he'd felt his heart leap and flick-flack. But what am I chasing here, he wondered, an 'engaged' unavailable pipe-dream ?

In the barge restaurant at a window dinner table for two, they decided on a vintage *cabernet sauvignon* from the wine list. By candlelight there seemed to be something very different about Lailla as she pointed beyond the window to the dome of St. Paul's Cathedral shrouded in a halo of floodlights. Close to St. Paul's on the darkening city skyline, Telecom Tower seemed heavily-laden carrying its bulk of radio dishes with the red warning flashes at its pinnacle. The river swept rapidly across the width of the window and then under Westminster Bridge.

"I know the exact place where Wordsworth composed his sonnet 'Upon Westminster bridge'," said Lailla. "I even know the date: 3rd September 1802." She smiled with pride to know this.

Traffic was flowing in a steady stream over the bridge onto each riverbank. The rows of cars were silent from this distance flowing onto the embankment which was lined with Victorian lamps and streamers of yellow light bulbs. Lailla tucked her hair behind one ear. When she touched her ring finger onto the stem of her filled wine glass, her mood turned serious.

"Have you noticed that I no longer wear an engagement ring ?" She glanced at her naked left hand.

Beyond a shrug of his shoulders, Mr Vodjani's diverted his eyes to her ring finger, although he felt little option but to disguise his degree of interest. Lailla drew closer as if sharing something suddenly personal between them, leaning forward.

"I couldn't mention it before," she admitted. "There was never a right moment during my driving lessons. Also..." She sat back, her expression appearing to wrestle with this issue beyond words. "...I was scared that my driving confidence would collapse into a horrible mess again."

Nervously she twirled the wine glass while looking out of the eye-level window.

"You don't have to explain. Really, you need not," said Mr Vodjani.

"No, I must !" Lailla confirmed this last opportunity with a voiced determination.

He studied her profile as she continued to look out the window as the power of the Thames flowing under the barge brought a shiver to the longboat and it swayed gently in the undertow, pulling at its moorings. Her stare remained fixed on the rapid waters as they glistened in the night. With some hesitation, while taking in a visible breath, she turned back to him.

"By the way what is your first name ?"

Mr Vodjani smiled. "Akram," he said.

Lailla nodded. She repeated the name 'Akram' quietly to herself. "Well Akram, early last year my English fiance, Robert, died in a car accident. Long before I commenced lessons with you. Have you any idea the

63

number of driving instructors and how many lessons I've begun and then given up on ? Do you know you are the first instructor who actually didn't break my driving confidence. You're the first one I've been able to talk to properly while driving a car." She nodded, lowering her eyes.

Mr Vodjani sat back astonished.

"So often those terrible memories of Robert's death in a car would well up and block me with fear..."

For some moments Mr Vodjani remained silent.

"I had no idea !" he confessed.

She laughed with open relief.

"Well considering this I'm glad I could help."

"No, Akram, it wasn't said in order for you to take it lightly." She touched his hand across the table between the wine glasses, interlinking a finger with his. Tilting her head, a strangely tragic and forlorn tenderness flushed on her cheeks. "This I will have you know is my first candlelit dinner with a man in a long, a very long time."

Lailla held up her glass as a toast.

"So can this be to us ?"

POINT OF IMPACT

    Out the corner of my eye, beneath a bridge far away on the distant curve of this motorway I dreamed for a moment of a cartwheeling motion, a splitting and fragmentation, a disintegration that was beyond me. Unnoticed or residually so, somewhere subconscious, because today I was alone and free with an empty road stretching ahead and an English summer sky drifting quietly above in its blueness.

A surge of pace as I sped along. Directed. Unworried. Just the feel of excitement for these holidays and the unfinished undergraduate project that I was speeding to continue: a university study on the coast, of monitoring marine limpet snails that would soon be re-emerging on the rocks at low tide. It was a scientific holiday at the beach. I checked the car speedometer and my wristwatch (on schedule for time) as the motorway began to curve towards a concrete flyover bridge.

Suddenly, there was the debris of a motorcar strewn clear across the road. It was too late to swerve as one of my front wheels hit a piece of headlamp lying on the tarmac and shattered it - I pulled right, sharply, to avoid hitting a twisted fender, and luckily I missed it. Then came the crunch of glass fragments and bits of plastic and oil under my wheels. I had little time to check for cars behind me in the rear-view mirror as I flattened a lone hubcap in the road and slowed down and steered out of this shrapnel of car pieces into the left-hand lane.

Passing under the motorway bridge I could see the epicentre of this mess in a buckled, stationary car with its occupants still inside ! It seemed like a hollywood scene. Surely this was a dream. Another rear-view check in the mirror showed no oncoming traffic, so I steered my vehicle back across the road lanes and onto the grassy middle island verge. I engaged brakes. Skidded not far away to a halt.

Silence. For some seconds I was dazed by the enormity of this situation... my heart a'thumping... TA DUM TA DUM TA DUM in my ears, becoming wrapped in an unreal eery state. I sensed myself in a kind of slow motion, a kind of sudden throbbing standstill of shock. TA DUM TA DUM TA DUM... as the heart valves pumped on loudly inside my chest and head. I closed my eyes and sat back into this reddened cardiac silence. This surreal state. An unbelieving state. It lasted until a bird twittered outside.

My camera for the science project was lying in its case on the dashboard, but I hadn't the cold calculation to take a photograph of this scene like a reporter, then try to sell the experience. Instead, I grabbed for a beach towel on the back-seat: the towel being my only first-aid equipment – how completely inadequate. I shouldered the car door open. To begin a run back towards the bridge, trying to recall my knowledge of pressure points of the body. My flimsy school knowledge of artificial respiration: how many breaths to administer per minute ? And the process of cardiac massage: I did remember that you need to place both palms of the hands firmly on the ribcage sternum and apply compression in short bursts of five.

With each anxious stride I took the concrete bridge got nearer. My vision seemed cloudy, it seemed almost mystical. I stopped running and blinked to clear my sight - yet nothing cleared - but there was no time to think except to take a few deep breaths: slowly inflating and deflating my lungs. That felt better. Yes, momentarily it felt better. I continued to walk rapidly, feeling very alone in my smallness along this grassy island verge with the beach towel slung over my shoulder, nearing a giant concrete pillar which supported the bridge: one pillar was behind another, and between, there protruding, was the buckled boot of the car. The rest of it was obscured.

Inwardly I forced myself to maintain the pace. Left. Right. Left. Right. While my gut rebelled. It seemed impossible, my hands were shaking with expectation and with fear, that this vehicle had come to a standstill wedged so tightly between those pillars and bounded front and back by the safety barriers which ran beneath the bridge along the motorway. It seemed ironic: those barriers to this car, one barrier of which the car had jumped right over and which now held it as securely as a baby fenced in a playpen - secure from any advance or retreat or further danger. As I rounded the pillar a whiff of oil, burnt rubber and death penetrated my nostrils and unknown to me, would be a smell that I still flinch from ten years later.

Squeezing between the bonnet and the motorway safety railing, I inched sideways through the narrow gap facing onto the car windscreen. To see a woman's face staring at me from the front passenger seat. There was no way to reach her passenger door which rested flush against the concrete pillar; so I climbed onto the bonnet of the car, lying stomach-down, and pulled myself up to the windscreen just a glass pane away from her face. She stared unblinking into my eyes. Her pupils were dilated. Her complexion a white-blue colour. A faint bruising could be seen on her forehead, but she was sitting straight and upright in her middle age with some tension in her muscles and a light rapid pulse at her neck.

WHOOOOOSH... a car suddenly sped past. My heart jumped out of this under-bridge silence. The passing car did not stop. Damn it ! Then another sound could be heard - a groaning, coming from beneath the steering wheel. A groaning and gurgling noise. I slid along the more buckled part of the bonnet and off where there was more space on the driver's side: enough for a back door on this side to be open. The driver's door was heavily damaged, staved in and jammed, but remarkably only this window-pane had shattered away. From front fender to tip of the open back door the paintwork was etched in long weals. I sniffed that acrid smell again. What was it ? Combined with my fear. For a moment my vision clouded over as I looked up, sighed, trying to empty my nostrils of this odour. Then I leaned over through the driver's broken window.

A grey-haired man lay crumpled on the floor. The old man was certainly the driver, all a'wheeze and gurgling. The man was stretched out below the steering wheel with his head resting beyond the gear-stick on the staring woman's feet. I could only reach into the window up to my waist, bending my torso, ever so careful not to shake the car too much (that staring woman may have a spine or neck injury) but I needed to get at him somehow.

"You all right guv ?" I asked.

His body was shaking in shock and turned away from me. Quite oblivious of anyone else, he continued his throaty gurgle. I was able to reach his foot at last and slip my hand under his trouser at the sock: the pulse felt rapid. He flinched, turned his head and spat a mouthful of blood onto the woman's leg. He saw me, I think, pull gently at his trousers.

"Can you get up," I prompted him.

He coughed, then slumped down.

In the background there was the sound of another car slowing on the motorway. But I had no time to worry about that. Not with this throaty man inside. I maneuvered myself back out of the window: the open rear door was another way in. I stepped to get around to it, into another scene - Sweet Mother of God !

Lying on the ground there was a quiescent third party. A second middle-aged woman as passenger in the backseat, peaceful as the first in a quiet sombre state though she was not staring nor sitting up. But draped half in, half out of the car, with her shoulders and head and one delicate arm resting on the sandy island. So peaceful. Oh, so solitary. Not even her mascara smudged; her red nail-polished hand pointing poetically, musically even in its whiteness, at the dust at her side. She was dead. There was no doubt of that.

I cast my eyes away in a dream-like state. I shivered inwardly and away from her seemingly untouched head that had seeped fluids of the brain into the soil. To see a uniformed nurse approach from that car recently stopped on the motorway, busy climbing over the safety barrier. I wiped moisture (if they were not tears) from my eyes... thankful to be pinched - by another person come to help - out of this lone dreamlike survey of the wreckage.

"Are you hurt ?" she questioned me.

"No. I wasn't in the car."

Glancing at the dead woman at my feet, the nurse's face paled.

"Quick help me," I urged the nurse impatiently, my vision become clear once again. "There's a man alive in front." I stepped over the other woman's body draped beautiful-unto-death and climbed onto the backseat and through to the front. The man continued to wheeze and spit blood.

"Ruptured lung I think," I called out.

The nurse came around to the driver's door and put her head through the shattered window.

I added: "There could be other internal injuries too."

"And that other woman ?" the nurse asked.

The face of the staring woman beside the driver seemed unchanged. But from close-up now I could even smell her pallor, and that blue bruised tinge, however faint on the forehead, looked more evil from this proximity. Then I saw her blink. Or was it just my imagination ? Those eyes almost blinked, or did they blink ? I leaned over and stared into them - deep black pools - like a naughty little schoolboy peeping nervously into a keyhole. Yet now I wanted to be noticed. Is anyone inside there ! Is anyone at home ? My shadow, it seemed, almost caused a minute pupil response in her eyes. Or did it ! Could it have ? And that feel of soft unconscious breath from her swollen lips. Her pulse was shallow... yes, but a pulse no less.

"She looks comatose," I told the nurse.

Then I moved my attention down to the bloodied floor and to the man gasping in his own delirium. But this time he did not flinch when I touched him. Somehow he was more focused on his breathing: a more concentrated need to wheeze small hiccups of breath into the damaged lungs, than respond to any of my worried words.

"Be careful with his ribs," the nurse warned.

I was equally careful not to bump the staring woman sitting unconscious in the front passenger seat, as my hands eased under the man's armpits. A movement which was made more difficult by the obstructive steering wheel and raised him spluttering into a seated posture on the floor. A soft, almost imperceptible whine (hardly a death-rattle, more a tired exhalation) made me turn to see the staring woman's head loll sideways and almost as suddenly, her eyes go glassy. Blocking us out of her depths. I waved my hands near her face.

"No, don't go !" I urged. "Hold on, for God's sake !"

But she didn't listen. She was far too eager to go glassy. Don't go... no, I held her shoulders tenderly, but she just flopped about. My heart thumping in my ears - my own heart. And that smell about - I couldn't stand it - an acrid smell. Why did you die in front of us ? For God's sake woman, we're here to help you ! I put my ear to her chest but all that could be felt now was a middle-aged coldness. I touched her lips with my fingers: no more soft shallow breathing. I was about to administer the kiss of life when...

"It's no use," the nurse cut in.

"What do you mean ?" I asked, with the staring woman still cradled in my arms.

"Look at her head. That deep fracture !"

Her lolling posture revealed a massive swelling under her hairline and skin on one side, the tinge of blueness belying the serious head injury beneath. I looked back at the nurse with moist eyes. She too had begun to feel the futility of our actions: wounds that were too serious to do anything about. Humbling us. Mocking us. As though something so much larger than our combined efforts was toying with life in front of us, snuffing it out like a thin flame. And we were just the observers - potentially also the victims - because it was sneering at us, showing us how tenuous our thread really is...

Which got me mad. I had to intervene. The man's body braced as I placed my wrists under his arms. Slowly I heaved him onto the seat. He spat and coughed again, red and frothy in a gush onto my hand, as I continued as if now driven by a madness to get him out of the car. Driven by a new strength to move him beyond these dead figures around us. I hauled him with movements that were as gentle as I could manage and he could cope with, between the front seats to the back; straining to cushion his broken ribcage and his head from the turns he and I had to make to exit, for which he seemed grateful. Then I hid his eyes, obscured their sight from the draped dead woman whom we had to step and pass over.

We laid him sideways in a recovery position still gurgling on the ground. He had become once again focused on easing soft gasps of air into his battered lungs. I checked his arms and legs for cuts - there was nothing noticeably serious - a few superficial lacerations and bruises, nothing else. The nurse reached for the beach towel which I had left on the car bonnet and placed it over the shivering that was this man's shock. She monitored his pulse. Before she shrugged at me: in a silent communication admitting that this was the best we could do in our capacity until further help arrived.

Crouching, I placed myself near the man's head and began to talk to him, to reassure this stranger of an elderly man, having myself seen the destruction around him - and yet he was quite unknowing of it. Who were these two women he had been driving, anyway ? Perhaps his wife in front ? Perhaps his neighbour in the back ? I continued to whisper reassurances into the ear of this man, who, in himself, was now merely living the function of his own lungs.

"Your name, please !"

I was tapped gently on the shoulder by a bobby. I stood up. The policeman's own face had paled, no doubt it was his own enormous shock of this scene, but he kept himself busy by writing my name and address neatly into a notebook.

"And may I have your telephone number ?"

I gave it to him, London code and all. Finally, the nurse and I could leave this scene of devastation to the wail of an ambulance siren approaching. The nurse exchanged a knowing glance with me. Then she came up and hugged me tightly. In the way we suddenly embraced, in its openness, its intimacy, I wondered whether that black-uniformed bobby would still believe our statement that we were just strangers caught up at an accident. But there was one more thing. I walked on over and in the privacy of my having been the first to witness the draped woman's face beautiful-unto-death, I quietly, respectfully covered her head with a cardigan. Her own cardigan which I found on the backseat where she had sat – an item of clothing untouched by the fury of the car accident, all soft and feminine and woollen white.

*

"Screw them ! I tell you, mate, screw them ! You're more important than their poxy undergraduate project. Leave it alone. Look at you... it's been almost a week since that accident and you're still staring at the world like a zombie."

I shrugged.

"Anyway, here's a mug of coffee."

"Thanks Tom."

He walked across the grass to get a battered deckchair, tossed out the dirt, and set it up beside mine. "Beautiful sunny morning though. That cherry tree is quite a sight, ain't it ? The way those blossoms bob in the air like clumps of snow with the bees buzzing around them."

77

I nodded at his description.

"When you're ready... you might like to read page seven." Tom pointed to the folded newspaper he had brought out and placed it in the deckchair. "Actually, I can't hang about. I've got to get back to campus to do some studying myself. Will you be OK ?"

"Yeh, mate, I'll be fine."

It ought to be said, I suppose in truth, that it was a lucky thing to have it happen at springtime. Of course I'm thinking about the car accident. So that instead of some stark and gnarl-branched winter scene I could now look at these blossomed trees in the increasing sun. Obviously those poor souls weren't lucky. Those two women involved fatally: I still can't bring myself to think about them with any degree of clarity. I've been stuck in this shell of shock staring at the world for days on end.

After the accident on that day, I drove straight back home here to student digs, jettisoning my project at the seashore. I left the project... quite unscientifically. I can't yet go back onto that motorway. I haven't yet even been able to get into a motorcar. Every now and then that man's face appears in my mind, a face spitting its blood, the face of that grey-haired man who survived: then it clouds over. The surprising thing is that at night I've had no nightmares. I sleep like the dead. I'm still waiting to be jolted by the experience, but it hasn't yet come. Only this glazed staring out across the unkempt, unmowed lawn during the day and that face appearing inside my head. Perhaps I'm going crazy.

I reached for the local newspaper.

SURVIVOR OF BRIDGE CRASH DIES

The five day fight for life of a 64 year old south London man has ended. Mr. E. V.Ferguson of Farnborough died last night in Croydon General Hospital of multiple injuries sustained in a car accident on Saturday. The crash occurred near Junction 6 of the M25, on the A22 southbound in Surrey. He was the only survivor of this fatal accident. Two other passengers in the car, his wife and his sister-in-law, died instantly. At the time police described the collision as a "tragic loss of life". It is thought Mr. Ferguson fell asleep at the wheel of his car travelling at high speed when it struck the pillars of a bridge overpass...

From this view a squirrel stood on the garden fence beyond the line of blossoms. I watched it angled on the fence, upright on its hindlegs, tail twitching, the sun striking the bushy fringe of its tail with a gleam of silver. I observed it while digesting the report of the car crash. Trying to digest the reporter's oversimplification of it. Both women did not 'die instantly'. The report in the newspaper is, I suppose, just an estimate. All the traumatic feelings I'd experienced are absent in the report because no one knows them except me: how I'd climbed up onto the car bonnet, stared through that windscreen at the lolling blue-faced woman in front, watched her breath ebb away...

My vision clouded briefly. Then beyond my blinking away of tears, the squirrel appeared still perched on the garden fence. Perhaps to the reporter it seemed as though both women had died instantly. To their relatives the newspaper report would be reassuring. And the man: the grey-haired man whose face was a living picture in my brain... the man who anonymously had coughed his red life's warmth onto my hand, with whom I had sweated and embraced in a bowed struggle to get out of that car. Now he had a name at last, down to his initials, even to his precise age and place of address. While all those facts of our struggle were left unsaid, unwritten, which remained secret and left for me as memories – as cloudy white and clumped as those waving blossoms.

The squirrel had descended the fence. Its jerky movements took it in a path through a bed of flowering yellow daffodils, while at intervals it sniffed and patted the soil, heading off across the lawn to the nearest cherry tree. Small black dots of bees were visible among the blossoms. One hanging cluster of white blossoms had attracted the attention of more bees than anywhere else. Busy they were, in their weaving flight, industrious in their role of being the principal pollinator. It was only with the playful shaking of some of these blossoms and a sudden buzzing frenzy of the bees that I noticed a cat in the tree tapping at a branch with its paw. The squirrel was unaware of the cat.

My senses suddenly alerted to this fact. As its hopping rodent movements with bush of flowing tail took the squirrel to the base of the tree. This whole unfolding scene then cramped in on me. It began to choke my senses. The sixty foot garden, of moderate length by London standards, was tiny by comparison to that motorway bridge overpass yet suddenly the lawn and rectangular wooden fence, the blossomed trees and flowerbeds, assumed a similarity and transformed in significance. Like a safe family car can transform into a trap; like a supporting bridge pillar becomes a point of collision. Yet instead of my vision clouding over again, it clarified, becoming as finely focused as that alerted cat itself amongst the white camouflaging blossoms.

I banged on the wood of my deckchair. But this warning went unheard.

"Shoo," I shouted. "Get away, shoo...!" My banging on the chair with curled fist was repeated.

But already the oblivious squirrel was half-way up the trunk of the cherry tree. It spiralled round, unluckily, reaching the level of the cat from an opposite side and even more obscured from it. My useless attempts at distraction had ceased. My eyes were transfixed: penetrating through to the impending point of collision in the tree as the cat stealthily bridged its way blossom-by-blossom, then it was blurred into a headlong acceleration of attack like a car on a motorway.

The point of impact of cat and squirrel occurred about where I envisaged it. The predator and rodent collided at a place of the trunk where it forked giving rise to three near horizontal branches. Momentarily I couldn't watch. It was as if that point of impact among cherry blossoms was colliding also inside my head. A blindspot it seemed at first. Then the spinning drop of the two creatures, two haired and four-legged creatures from the white canopy of blossoms of the tree, redrew my attention. It was the hysterical tumbling motion that re-focused me.

When they struck the ground they were still locked in claw and tooth. The pit of my stomach had assumed a snuffed-out-life-force feeling. A dread of the inevitability of

82

violent death-by-force. It was almost a numbing feeling were it not for the flick of a bushy tail as the squirrel began to fight back, after a jump and splayed cartwheeling, which caused the cat to halt as a rodent claw swiped into its fur and spinal hackles. The injured squirrel limped off. But as it was again confronted, it spiralled into another defence, struck the cat on its whiskered chin and this time the squirrel claw sank deep. The cat was stunned. Hurt. It shook its head. Neither could I believe, at first, this intense rodent desperation for life. While the cat weaved its head to-and-fro, bloodied and held low to the ground. I watched as the cat slunk away - countered and foiled in its attack.

"Hah, hah !" My laugh echoed within the space of my brain. With a loudness that caught me completely off guard. It was like a backward death-rattle all of my own. It happened as I watched the squirrel climb to safety up onto the fence. Then the rodent chattered an alarm call across the garden, its rapid tail-sweep illuminated with silver in this light.

And for the first time in almost a week, ever since that car accident, as the squirrel limped its victorious way along the fence… I realized it wasn't all that bad. I had just laughed out loud. Wonderful. Damn fine squirrel.

Critter that it was - it had poked death in the face and survived !

When I walked into the house I knew, however difficult it would be to drive along the motorway past the accident site, that low tide was just an hour away and I was ready to load my scientific gear back into the car.

LOVE IN AN ENGLISH GARDEN

An English affair
of wicker chair
and royal Dalton porcelain,
Major Robert Harquin
nodded for a cup of tea.

Lady O'Connor
did the honour
with a delicate wrist,
added a biscuit twist
after the spot of cream.

A glorious spring
ring-a-ding-ding
she admired that moustache,
his manners weren't gauche
at their little table for two.

Iced her perrier
introduced the terrier
beside a Burnet rose,
the cherry blossom grows
and the grass is manicured.

Her glistening hair
in scented air
the Major extracted his snuff,
a savoury pinch was enough
he dusted his hands clean.

When he sneezed
seemed quite pleased
the terrier cocked an ear,
tail-wagged, it was clear
that doggie had become excited.

Circling his shoe
What to do ?
Lady O'Connor embarrassed,
her guest was being harrassed
by a terrier in love.

Doggie blue
mounted the shoe
Lady's: "I beg your pardon",
the Major coughed: "Ahem !"
to love in an English garden.

SOFTDRINKS AND CANTEEN LADIES

Sitting put in our chassis raised high off the tarmac we listened to the engine in silence, hoping nothing was wrong, as our vehicle heaved and spluttered and grunted mechanically at low speed as it took us out of the storage depot. Grunting under the judder of an engine still cold and bunged up from a night of standing outside in the depot yard, shuddering heavily under weight of our ten ton softdrinks load.

Behind us was the low-peaked warehouse with orders of softdrinks stacked outside on wooden pallets and half a dozen other trucks lined up waiting their turn to be loaded. The fork-lift cars, one man perched precariously on each of these dodgem-vehicles, were weaving a path ludicrously fast from warehouse to truck like bees encircling and pollinating a flower. Each pallet of softdrinks released onto the truck in-waiting jerked the suspension sideways as a load landed, the truck groaned on its bearings, sank lower and heavier until like us after the side-flaps were clipped and clicked shut, revved out a belch of night oil and inched its way forward onto the motorway.

Time of morning when one's brain is cleared by the sounds of birdsong; by dawn-light casting pastoral shades of pink onto the clouds, purpling the English sky as we gradually picked up pace. Jim was beside me in our chassis of glass. He as the driver. Between us on the seat lay a folder which enclosed fifteen delivery slips. Jim blinked out of the windscreen at the haze of road ahead - few cars at this time of morning – from Enfield we were soon speeding on the M25 outskirts of London beside pastures where cows stood fat and half-asleep in a sea of green grass. Beyond them the wheat was laid out smooth and thick in fields of rectangles with hedgerows. It wasn't long before strands of early morning traffic began to whizz past.

"Where to today Jim ?" I asked. The words echoed in our glass compartment. Jim seemed surprised at my sudden intrusion - taken from the depths of thought or tiredness or something weighing on his mind from the night before. He gestured at the bulky paperwork on the seat.

"Have a look, mate."

I took the blue folder. Opened it.

"So what's this... new delivery slips ?" They were dot-matrix computer printouts each with the customer's address, the softdrinks order in crates or trays, the total weight in fraction of tons, an outlined box at the corner of each page in which to mark the empty bottles returned, and a place for the signature of both customer and driver.

"21st flaming century. That's what it is," Jim quipped ruefully while squinting out of the windscreen at the glare of morning sun. He reached for a pair of sunglasses on the dashboard and donned them. "We'll soon need a flipping degree in computers to keep up with this job."

There were fifteen such invoices, collated and stacked according to vicinity. Jim had already plotted our quickest delivery route today - through St. Albans, Bushey, Hemel Hempstead. We'd worked a few times before, Jim and me, though by no means were drivers and mates like us fixed into teams: particularly among contract worker's like us, placement each day was random. Sometimes we were kept together intermittently as partners for one travel route a couple of times a week, but only because of our previous co-ordinated knowledge of where to deliver the drinks down narrow country roads and along backstreet alleyways of villages and hamlets. This was one of those times: I had last been with Jim three days ago.

Our conversation veered onto the latest scores of England in the 1990 Football World Cup. This finding of common ground, these shared interests were necessary because of their role in drawing us closer for the work soon at hand. To break the ice of our linking up as a team once again; to familiarise ourselves with the mate with whom we would labour over this day. In a short space of time we must trust each other implicitly.

"Reckon it'll be a long day ?" I flicked through the delivery slips once more, then placed them back between us on the vinyl seat.

"We could finish by three o'clock."

"That's not too bad."

"Depends..." Jim glanced at me from the speeding white line on the road more than a man's height below us. "Depends on how many small customer's. It's Friday you know."

I nodded. Small customers. He could see I understood.

Shortly we arrived at the first drop. It was a pub. Jim deftly maneuvered the metal bulk of the truck half onto the pavement next to the cellar hatch. We slipped on heavy-duty gloves, and jumped from the cab. I unclipped the curtain-flaps and slid the canvas open on the side of the truck facing the cellar. Our packaged load was shoulder-height with softdrinks: cans, baby bottles, slim bottles, 1.5 litre, 2 litre, 10 litre bag-in-a-box and high-pressure cannisters. Jim climbed onto a pallet in the back of the truck, invoice in hand, and stripped off to his vest. He looked at the upstairs pub windows. No one seemed to be awake. We decided to unload their order first. To wake this small customer later.

Time for that mutual trust. The co-ordination of limbs and sureness of eye. The need to develop a rhythm together, the reflex to catch trays of 24 cans or as many bottles lobbed in mid-flight: I raised my gloved hands to an upward stretch ready to pivot on my hips and lower the volleyed package onto the pavement. Jim located the first item on the list.

"Item 1, baby bottles, five crates of..." he called.

"Aye," I confirmed and they came on down.

One, two, three, four, five in flight.

91

Jim's role, he knew, was to let each crate fly free as near to the horizontal as possible. That way it landed flat and solid, the only sound in my ears was Jim's displacement of the right crate from the piles on the truck and the hard 'twack' as it connected in my gloved grasp. Its flight was soundless. The morning traffic was now beyond our concentration.

"Item 2, slim bottles, two crates of..."

"Yo !" I said ready to turn upwards.

They continued to come heavily: item 3, item 4, item 5 (?) until three stacks of crates chest-high encircled the cellar hatch, with a few miscellaneous packages topping them. Theirs was not a large order.

Jim jumped deftly down off the truck. He located the pub front door and rang the bell. The place was deserted. Not even a sniffing dog around. I peered inside a yellow tinted window to see all remnants of last night there: glasses on the counter marked with dried beer; butt-filled ashtrays; a dart on the floor fallen off a dartboard in one corner; upholstered chairs pulled out from around tables and facing the exit as if everyone had left suddenly in some headlong rush for sleep or more entertainment. Jim rang the bell repeatedly. No one stirred. No dog barked. We looked up at what appeared to be bedroom windows on the first floor.

I shouted: "Drinks delivery - open up !"

As Jim rang the bell again, then banged on the stained glass of the front door. An upstairs window was suddenly pushed ajar and a man's face appeared, dishevelled and sleepy, at its opening.

"What the hell you doing here so early ?"

"Delivery mate," said Jim.

"Do you know what frigging time it is !"

"Sorry mate, nothing written down on the delivery slip."

"Quarter-to-bloody-eight in the morning," the man glowered down upon us, unshaven and furious with lack of sleep. "This is a pub, this is, open late, not some bloody sweetshop on the corner !"

He disappeared behind the curtains as Jim rolled his eye-balls at me, then quipped:

"First satisfied customer of the day."

Not unexpectedly it was the publicans missus that came down in her gown and slippers to open the cellar hatch for us. She apologized meekly for her husband's outburst; likewise we struck up friendly conversation while she stood by uninhibited and curlered in the morning light, watching me slide crates down the wooden ramp to Jim now in the depths of the cellar.

"End of the week you know," she explained, glancing up at the curtained windows. "And he's got another heavy one on tonight."

"That's all right love."

I was between sliding one tray of cans down the shute and moving the next stack of crates closer to the hatch.

"Just that we're contract workers, you know. We don't have much to do with the ordering or when its to be despatched unless you request it from the company and they print it on the slip."

She nodded: "Right. I'll tell him." Her tone was slightly embarrassed.

"Item 5 out of stock," Jim called from the cellar.

"Again !" she cried indignantly, with a pained look on her face, knowing that after we leave she will have to inform her hung-over man upstairs of this. "But they didn't deliver it last time either !"

I shrugged my shoulders. She sighed, hands on her hips.

There was nothing to say in this or in the fact that their order should have been here yesterday. In the early days this status of impotence used to affect me more. At first I used to curse being in this daily firing-line: merely a working-class cog in some other man's wheel of fortune.

There we were, the two of us, Jim and myself, standing daily in front of this volley of small-customer dissatisfaction like two cogs closest to the face of a giant clock; the one's who were confronted first by the time-keeper and blamed for any problem in the inner workings.

Almost as if when companies get as big as this one has grown there is an inevitable fraying at the edges where the little men, us, the delivery men, are left to passify those fringe customers who in their smallness (only 12 crates please, they ask) are powerless in the bigger scheme of things. Jim and I dealing with the overflow of these tiny payers by appeasing them with "item 5 next time" – we reply, politely.

"It's jungle law," Jim piped up when we were back in the chassis and on the road heading towards our next drop.

"What ?" I turned to him.

"I can see your mind ticking over," said Jim. "And I know what you're thinking." He could see the early morning start to the day on my face. Somehow I always sided with the downtrodden.

"Doesn't make it easier on that poor old geyser we've just left," I said.

"Come on mate," Jim changed the subject. "Ain't she luvely," he pointed to a woman in a mini-skirt assuming a voluptuous pose at a bus stop.

Indeed, in the morning light she seemed quite beautiful, although Jim's forthright sexism irked me. It was still so early and yet Jim and I were already drawing together as a unit. I decided that it must have been that throwing of crates, or the angry customer, or our passifying of the wife, or the mutual solidarity we both felt at being small and insignificant like that pub owner. Probably it was all these things. Jim knew better than me, he was the easier joker and the freer-flier.

"Cor blimey, look at that !" he exclaimed.

Riding on a bicycle ahead of us was a young, flamboyant apparition of a man. With knees pumping at right angles outward from his pedals he weaved away from the parked cars lining the street straight into our path. His hair was shaved bald on the sides and back with a fountain tuft ontop tied in a bow and a lonely fringe at his neckline. He wore luminous yellow sunglasses and West African shorts and vest in an ethnic print of green and cerise.

"Full marks for originality," said Jim.

And in my introspective frame of mind, that seemed exactly it. Just like this bicycle man, Jim and I too had to choose a way to forget ourselves each day, forget this smallness, insignificance, in the flamboyance of some other behaviour. So we threw jokes at each other: about the bigger customers that whinged and whined; the diabolical traffic we met along the way; that aging sex worker on the street corner that, Jim reckoned, still loved herself but, as he unkindly said, looked more pricked than a second-hand dartboard. In between he turned up the music of Capital radio. Our eyes were ever in search of cool street-walking beauties... we were almost extravagant at this admiration and this distraction. And then, of course, there were also the canteen ladies: but not yet, we haven't come to them, but we will.

First we had to bury ourselves in our softdrinks workload. Work in which we demonstrated efficiency in our strength and rhythm of pace, though sometimes our politeness did wane. In a haze of biceps straining, sweaty armpits and sleeve-wiped forehead and calloused hands, we seemed like a two man conveyor belt of hips pivotting as arms stretched up to the truck then swung down to the pavement in a softdrink arc of crates.

"Item 19 - coming down."

"Item 23, item 24, item 16."

To be wheeled on a barrow (six crates at a time or nine trays of cans) into cinemas, snooker and bingo halls,

97

bottle-stores, cafe's, restaurants, police stations. Down the hatch at pubs. Across factory floors. Lugging the weight up stairs we stopped for a stolen moment, looked at each other panting for breath - got the slip signed and then moved on. Sometimes when Jim looked at me I knew that he was thinking about this being another flaming place without a lift !

Though in all this I was never far away from wanting, somehow, to ease those small customers. Nagging thoughts admittedly they were. Maybe coming more from a need in myself: to ease my own feeling of being dispensable, of being insignificant as a menial contract worker in a giant and modern company.

"Hullo boys."

We arrived at the aforementioned canteen. Our delivery of softdrinks was wheeled in as we were met by shrivelled and spindly old Dora in her white apron and cap.

"I see you parked your broom outside today, Dora," Jim entered jokingly.

"Oooh, you horror, you are Jim."

"Where does it go love ?" Jim glanced down at the barrow he was hauling. I followed close behind with my own six crate load.

Dora pointed to the storeroom: "Put it anywhere. As long as it's inside."

"Naughty, naughty... Dora," Jim twisted her words into a sexual connotation and the dear old woman's face crinkled and blushed as she turned to Maggie, also dressed in the same fashionless white outfit, who had overheard this last exchange of words and was chuckling to herself. There we were - sweaty, tired, come through the service entrance over drains with crates of stinking empties waiting for us – and we had been met by two uncompromisingly happy faces.

"You both look tired," Maggie said coming on over.

I nodded as I took off the heavy-duty gloves and wiped my forehead on my sleeve. Maggie must have sensed something in my eyes because she looked at me, lowered her voice, and said confidingly:

"Thank God you're here. We were near dying for a drink."

Then in his inimitable style Jim began to chat them up. "Not half a good smell that !" I heard him say. And Dora made a move over to a stainless steel pot and ladled out some thick brown stew and carrots for us. She plopped a dollop of mashed potato on each plate. We perched on stools, Jim and me, in a corner of this humid, stark, windowless kitchen as these two old dears clucked around us trying to ease the stretched tiredness from our bones.

"Where's Polly ?" I asked.

"She left us," said Maggie.

"Really. Polly has left ! Why ?"

"Some Prince Charming came and swept her off her feet. Or so she said. She's following him out of London up into the East Midlands somewhere. Can't say I blame her. I'd do the same given the chance."

Looking at Maggie, then at Dora, I realized that our conversation seemed to brighten up their spirits and their whole demeanour, it gave them a short respite from the mindless washing of dishes and endless spooning of soups or pouring of gravies. They too were taken away from the thankless monotony, the crying smallness of their job. It was like a sudden party among old friends. With Jim and me in our own way demonstrating to them equally how important they were to us. At last we left them and wheeled our barrows (now full of crated empties) back to the truck.

After departing there was no need yet to switch on the radio music in our chassis. Nor even to throw each other a volley of jokes. Instead, Jim and I drove off from the canteen well fed and for a while silent, no longer intent on ogling the vibrant street-walking women, lost more in the strange glow of comfort given to us by Dora and Maggie. Our faces having suddenly been noticed behind the barrows.

As if no one else today more than those white-dressed canteen ladies had so evenly matched - the tired, plodding, endless smile that we must pass to the customer. Them in their job of filling the hungry stomach. And us quenching by our particular softdrink intervention: the thirst of this English nation. In them Jim and me end this day easier...

"See you tomorrow, mate."

"Tomorrow then Jim. Ta-ra."

THE GARBAGE COLLECTOR

When Edward Sunningham stepped between the entrance pillars he felt dwarfed by the imposing columns as he passed them by heading out down the stone steps and into the British Museum courtyard, then made his way through and beyond the entrance gates. Today his mind felt tired, his head was throbbing lightly from too much reading. Knowing however that there were only two more research days to go, comforting himself with this thought, he silently nursed this library headache as he went.

On this penultimate lunch-break Edward had decided unusually to take leave of this workplace. He needed a breath of fresh air. Imagining that not before long he would be high-speeding, by InterCity rail, to a well-earned holiday on the west coast of Cornwall. The prospect of this holiday break had an urgency for which he almost could not wait.

True enough, this fortnight of research here in the British Library had been intriguing for him. It was a fascinating place in which to do research. In fact so unparalleled a museum as to be the reason why, all those previous lunchtimes, Edward had wandered with an empty stomach through its vast expanse to visit the variety of exhibits on display. Walking the great halls of artefacts. Burying himself in ancient tombs of mummies instead of eating in the cafetaria, wandering through Mycenean and Ming ages, through rooms of ancient Etruscan figures and Roman oil lamps. Especially room number thirty in the east wing – which he decided was his favourite – with its handwritten historical diaries, major British novels written in quill and ink, immortal romantic poetry scribbled in haste, and letters penned by the greatest names in English literature.

But today Edward stepped outside. As he drew away from the sculpted pediment of the building he walked with a purpose, at an almost strolling pace, with a kind of soft-muscled athleticism that was the most he could muster to escape that cloistered library atmosphere from which he had come. His headache was an encumbrance to going any quicker. Edward found that holding his head slightly back in a rather awkward posture, as one does to sniff the swirling autumn smells, helped to arrest the light throbbing of his head. And once he was breathing the air deeply – he felt at last all measure of books, the unreality of words and sentences and reams of research paragraphs he had plodded through - begin to dissipate.

When finally Edward shut his eyes, he had finished a tuna and coleslaw sandwich whilst sitting on a bench in a Bloomsbury park. The relaxing environment here was interrupted by little more than the cooing of doves and a distant hum of cars, which he ignored, behind Georgian buildings which surrounded this park. So too did he ignore the rummaging of a blackbird among fallen leaves nearby. Edward sighed behind closed eyelids. The sunlight struck his face with an even warmth. Inwardly, Edward smiled to himself, pleased at having made this lunchtime choice.

"Hullo guv. Name's Harry."

A voice emerged uncomfortably close to Edward's ear. Someone - a man - had sneaked up beside him like an ear-kissing phantom without his even noticing. And any reply to this anonymous man became lost in...

"Was down in Soho just a moment ago," the man wheezed to Edward in a genial, confiding tone. He crinkled a handful of plastic bags which he was carrying. "To get some of these carriers," he confirmed to Edward. "And there I was just minding my own business in Brewer Street, City of Westminster," the man curled his tongue around this last tongue-twisting word. "And do you know what I see for sale in a window?"

By this time Edward's eyes were fully open but not quite focused, his head turned to this blurred fuzzy vision. He shrugged at it.

"Well there I am, guv, and in this shop window I read: chocolate willies for sale. Below them advertised are low calorie edible panties in a strawberry flavour; peppermint condoms also; and will you believe it... will you believe it... lager-flavoured nipple cream ! Now this is something I scratch my head about you know like. So in I go and there's this tall bosomy missus at the counter and I says to her: I didn't know you'd become a restaurant establishment ? Suddenly this missus gets all huffy with me and I'm out like a bloomin' shot cause she's calling for this bouncer."

Edward smiled at this bundle of a talkative man beside him, a man fully engrossed in his own conversation. This man who went by the name Harry continued:

"Now I'm not one to be fobbed off easily. Not me mate," he shook his bearded profile vigorously. "Anyway I want to know what all these flavours mean. So I step inside the next but one shop – almost next door like - to ask about those strawberry concoctions, chocolate and peppermint things just out of interest, like. And do you know what the bloke in the other shop does ? He takes me aside as if he believes he knows what I want, walks me past shelves of a hundred different porno books. You don't want that - he says to me regarding those flavours - and points at video cassettes on a revolving stand. Special for you today - Sir - at twenty pounds each, today's special just for you... straight, gay, bondage or bizarre, he says. These hard-core videos are exactly what you need."

Edward straightened up against the park bench as the scraggy man leaned even closer.

"Now can you believe that, guv !"

Again, Edward shrugged at him, feeling at a loss how to answer this candid stranger who was asking him – if not challenging him – to reveal his personal views of sexual morality.

"Don't you tell me what I need, I says to that Brewer Street shop bloke, pointing my finger into his chest. Hardcore videos - pah !" Harry turned away. "Those porno people make me sick."

As suddenly as he had arrived, the man named Harry then started to get up from the bench. And off he walked. Edward watched him ambling, a lone figure moving away with his shoulders hunched like someone's father or grandfather gone astray. A pensioner is what he resembled to Edward, around about that age somewhere between sixty and sixty five with not a smell of alcohol about him and too groomed to be homeless. Or perhaps, Edward thought, groomed was the wrong word for his appearance, for someone who at least attempts to curtail the dishevelment that can happen to a lonely person of his age. Dressed in a chequered coat of cinnamon colour, a green flat-cap on his head at a jaunty angle, and a pair of old navy-blue flares tied up with a belt. As he made off, his hunched gait and an umbrella helped to balance a leg that was disabled and lame: the sideways-facing foot being dragged along like a toppled mast.

Harry stopped. Not too far away for Edward to discern what he was up to. Edward got the feeling that this man of upright morality was about to return, but that was not so, it was merely him pausing to pull the disabled leg around for support. Then he hung his umbrella on one angularly bent arm in order to extract a plastic carrier bag from his coat pocket, threaded the straps of the bag along his folded arm so that the bag was hanging and open, duly unhooked the umbrella from its dangling position and continued to head off.

Along a path which ran the circumference of the park; a gravel walkway bound on the outside by London plane trees and on the inside by a rolling lawn. There were no shrubs to obstruct Edward's view of him, even to the furthest perimeter, as Harry gravelled his noisy way along. It became evident then that he was searching the path ahead. Which gripped Edward's attention, of course, onto what he might be looking for. As though he had lost something: so intent were his sideways glances, his sweeping vision. When at last he recognised an object on the ground, Harry turned and headed obliquely across the path in a direct line towards it.

Steering himself until his dragging rudder of a leg caught onto a cheese and onion crisps packet and pulled it along with him. Harry stopped at the path's outer edge, speared a wrapper with the spike of his umbrella, then speared an empty cigarette box, then something else soft and tissue-like. This completed, he lifted the brolly up to the bag dangling off his arm and disimpaled the garbage into it. The crisps packet at his foot was still engaged to be dragged along as he continued away and now steered the disabled leg into a scrap of discarded cling wrap.

A clock chimed nearby...

"Damn," Edward muttered to himself. He had to return to his library research in the domed reading room. The bearded old man at the other end of the park collecting garbage did not notice Edward get up from the bench, nor did he notice Edward leave the Bloomsbury park.

*

Today, the final day of Edward's project in the British Museum library, meant that his holiday on the coast of Cornwall was merely a matter of hours away. He relished the thought. Except that after that visit to the park yesterday, contemplating it seriously overnight, there was one extra thing he felt he must attend to.

Those events yesterday in the park had actually disturbed Edward. As if a splinter had pushed under his skin and penetrated. Yesterday's experience with Harry had afterwards felt as if some foreign element had jabbed through into his moral conscience, enough to become embedded. Enough for him to feel the need to needle it out and examine this foreign wedge at close-quarters. To speak to that old man – Harry - who expressed such moral uprightness to him, a stranger who had confided in Edward and he now couldn't believe how aloof he had been in return.

All right, he assured himself, so perhaps at the time my mind was too stuffed with books to the point of tiredness or outward insensitivity. But whatever explanation, Edward felt spurred on enough yesterday afternoon and this morning to make sure he completed the last of his research early in order to spend a few hours back in that Bloomsbury park. At least from lunchtime onwards. To clear away this issue of conscience. Speak to the old man - Harry - shake his hand at least, introduce himself, and thus draw out that splinter-of-conscience before his Cornwall holiday began. Edward hoped that this time of a few hours would be enough.

Back at the Bloomsbury park 'their' bench was empty. He looked around but there was no sign of Harry. Other faces were recognisable from yesterday: the businessman reading a sporting magazine a few benches away, and that woman on the lawn sketching. Edward decided to take a walk around the park himself. To get some exercise while he ate a pickled-fish sandwich, before he sat down to wait. It had been a mild end of September in London. The trees showed traces of autumn in their darkening russet shades and a free-fall of leaves had begun. Edward guessed that that artist woman cross-legged on the grass with her wooden tray of pastels may be trying to capture these autumn foliage colours of yellow and deep ochre.

Underfoot the crunch and crackle of fallen leaves brought back to Edward's mind the picture of Harry using his disabled mast-of-a-limb to drag along garbage. It seemed peculiar, Edward thought, having never spoken to the man, to now consider him so fluently by first-name. A squirrel suddenly crossed the path a short distance ahead to the amusement of a young boy, it flicked its tail as the boy approached, before spiraling up a tree. More people were entering the park: so Edward speeded his pace to get back to 'their' bench still unoccupied. He threw the last crusts of his sandwich to a clambering flock of pigeons on the lawn. Then took off his corduroy jacket, loosened his tie, undid the top button of his shirt, and sat down to wait.

Until the lunch-hour drifted by and suddenly ended. Until the park drained of all but a handful of tourists (many probably from the British Museum like him) and three homeless men smoking together on the grass. There was still no sign whatsoever of the old man, no emergence yet of Harry. The novel Edward had unpacked for a distracting read he placed back into his black leather briefcase together with his reading glasses, when he remembered that those three homeless men on the grass had also been here yesterday: they may well have seen Harry earlier on today.

Edward crossed over to them.

"Excuse me. Might I have a word ?" he asked, interrupting their passing around of a cigarette. The smoker holding the filter-less cigarette quickly stole another deep drag on it.

"Aye, sure mate," said one of them, and gestured at the lawn beside him. "Sit down !" Edward walked around to the vacant space between them and sank to his haunches, placing his briefcase on the grass. The other two examined Edward with interest; there was a sour, almost intoxicating odour of alcohol about. They exchanged names and it appeared that the one man gaining most time on the cigarette - Bert - was their spokesman, eager to hear what Edward had to say for himself.

Edward spoke directly to him. "I was wondering if you'd seen someone here this morning. An elderly man with a bad leg. Name of Harry ?"

"Mean that geyser who's barmy about litter."

"That's right, yes," Edward said, nodding at this obvious and accurate identification.

The homeless man looked at his friends and shook his head with some amusement. "You missed it earlier on: a real right hoot it was, weren't it just something boys ?" The homeless man slapped the shoulder of the smoker next to him as the third chuckled and smiled toothlessly. "He got taken off in an ambulance, he did, about two hours ago."

Edward frowned, moving a bit closer.

"What happened ?"

"It's not the first time either - I reckon. There he was on his round, y'know, round the park like, dragging half the rubbish in the world with his gammy foot and stabbing at things with his umbrella," said Bert who rolled his eyeballs mockingly at the sky. "Anyway, there were these two young lads walking closeby - skinheads, weren't they boys ? You know... the rough Tower Hamlets type. They threw a newspaper into the flowerbed over there. So ol'

113

Harry calls: 'Oiy, please pick that up !' And most times skinheads don't like to be spoken to by old folks anyway. Next thing there's this scuffle and Harry's lying on the ground punched in the face, bleeding from the nose but still waving an outstretched arm and shouting: 'Pick it up ! Pick it up !'"

"Goodness," said Edward, his voice shaken. He shifted his haunched weight onto another foot. "What hospital was he taken to?"

"Can't say."

Bert looked to the others. Neither did they know.

"Was he hurt badly ?"

"Let me tell you guv, he'll do fine. Ol' Harry's a tough one." The homeless man whom his friends called Bert leaned over and confided in a low and acrid-smelling voice: "Between you and me, can't say I've met a nicer bloke. Says he can't stand living by a park he calls a tourist pigsty. This park being so near the British Museum and all those foreigners eating their lunches here. He's been carting rubbish out of this place for years - lives nearby, somewhere in Bloomsbury - though I don't know where." Bert discarded his cigarette butt on the lawn with a deft flick of his finger: "Got a fag for us, guv."

Edward stood up. He walked over and picked up the discarded butt, then conscientiously placed it in a nearby litter bin. He handed the three homeless men two cigarettes each, before departing. And began his walk to Tottenham Court Road tube station to catch an underground train home where he would prepare for his Cornwall holiday. While walking Edward couldn't help noticing for the first time on the way to the tube station - all the garbage strewn in these particular side streets and the people going about their business avoiding, or stepping over it, pretending not to notice.

PAVAROTTI IN HYDE PARK

(30th anniversary of his career)

Umbrella'd against incessant rain,
we stand sandwiched in a huddle
of a hundred thousand people

undulating on this bluegrass lawn,
human waves sway fish-like
in a darkening quagmire.

A Prince and Prime Minister sit
beyond my barrier of eyelids,
I'm closed to an inner mood

to the drip of water off my nose,
as this tenor of drizzling night
cradles an aria by Verdi.

Libretto's wash over this audience
which stun and head-tilt us
in crinkling raincoats.

Announcement: "Pavarotti will claim
the heart of London tonight !" is
simulcast worldwide

to Ponchielli, Wagner's Lohengrin
exploding a thunderous applause,
while the foot puddle grows

in massed choir prickling the flesh
of *Tosca*, eerily a flute sighs
over the theatre pediment.

A tuxedoed man distant on-stage
is that tiny morsel of bait
hooking this crowd

from Carmen to *Mamma* I changed
weight onto another foot,
then glanced around

at people become opera quietened
to *Nessun Dorma*: his finale
of virtuoso gooseflesh.

THIS SEASON'S ROCK
(Bands on the beat: Summer 1991)

A sudden Sting into the beat
been rasped into a Vital Groove,
AC DC make this beat
Beach Boys, Bee Gees
take this beat
with New Fast Automatic Daffodils.

Choose Blodwyn Pig, Wishbone Ash
Joe Cocker or Whitney Houston,
a Blip Culture
with Combo Cabana,
Everly Brothers or Deborah Harry.

Hammersmith Odeon, T&C Club
gives Slow Bongo Floyd
and Buzzcocks a buzz:
MC Hammer, Transvision Vamp
take the beat
make the beat.

Bug Kann and the Plastic Jam
Shirley Bassey in the Albert Hall
Placido Domingo at Covent Garden
a Pelican Retorts
the Candy Skins.

Elvis Costello and Vanilla Ice
UB40 in Finsbury Park
Earls Court too
will take this beat,
with Manic Street Preachers
and Jungle Jazz.

Linton Kwesi Johnson's dub begins
King Pleasure and the Biscuit Boys
Silent Emotions
and a Mushroom Attack,
as Rod Stewart with Status Quo.

Gloria Estefan and Gipsy Kings
is Paul Simon a Pet Shop Boy ?
take the beat with ELO
Enuff Z'Nuff
in London.

SCRATCH OF THE POLTERGEIST

Helen leaned back on the continental pillow, touching a finger to the pale brown envelope, stroking and enjoying the manilla feel of it, before turning the envelope face up to re-confirm that it was really her name. Yes, the letter was addressed to her. *'Ms. H. Edwards'* was printed in bold for all to see above the Southwark address near London Bridge. Smiling with a self-congratulatory smile, she murmured to herself:

"From Hell, Hull, Halifax… they've finally found me a room. I can move my belongings out of here at last."

Slowly she exhaled a sigh of relief. When Helen refolded the acceptance letter she was unaware that she had read it through three times in quick succession, unaware that she was fingering the saving grace of this sheet of official paper as she began to relax into thoughts of her new student accommodation and the long awaited independence she deserved.

Cross-legged on the white futon which had served as her bed these last eleven weeks, she glanced across the length of the split-level apartment which belonged to her uncle Stuart. Her gaze ran to its high-arched windows overlooking the river Thames below. Finally her student dossing down on other people's lounge floors was over, this exploiting the hospitality of family and friends beyond what she felt was reasonable. Her eyes scanned the clean perspective of varnished oak floorboards all the way up to a raised open-plan dining area. This apartment had an affluence easily afforded by her city stockbroker uncle but which she doubted she would ever be able to attain herself. In this spacious riverside apartment she had always felt entirely the guest; now she would happily and not before time relieve Uncle Stuart of her prolonged presence.

Helen smiled to herself as it struck her, and it seemed quite ridiculous in this circumstance of finally receiving the college letter, to declare that phrase: 'From Hell, Hull, Halifax'. A bizarre and outdated medieval triangle of words. Yet during this lounge floor period the medieval of London had become a rather intimate part of her life. The riverside apartment was a stone's throw from Tooley Street, and she had exploited its proximity to entertain her afternoon hours before cello practice at home. Helen had purchased a season ticket to visit the eerie London Dungeon museum. To feed a childhood passion she always remembered having for the macabre, the afterlife, death and the supernatural. On display in the London Dungeon museum were actors as well as life-like models of medieval peasants and famous aristocracy alike being stretched, hung, drawn-and-quartered in a dark torture house. In memory of England's grotesque and gory past. Where witches and traitors centuries ago were sentenced without mercy to be burned at the stake, and as a last plea would cry for deliverance: 'From Hell, Hull, from Halifax !'

"What earthly reason did you have to buy a season ticket to the London Dungeon ?" Uncle Stuart had asked Helen condescendingly, a wry smile curling the corner of his mouth.

She ignored him. Determined this time that she would not respond to his tendency to ridicule. She felt

122

tired of having to justify her interest in unexplained phenomena and disturbances of the past. Disturbances which often had a supernatural element. Initially Helen defended her fascination for the occult because she was a guest in his apartment and she felt obliged not to be rude. Explaining why she felt the need to explore and read about mystical or spiritual phenomena, however sceptical his expression turned to her in reply.

"You don't really believe in Tarot cards, Helen ?"

"Why not ? Anyway, it's not just a matter of blind faith. I won't simply dismiss the use of Tarot cards."

Eyebrows raised, again he smiled his condescending smile. She would fold her arms defensively, thinking what a shame her uncle believed everything was reducible to the rational, that only science held the answer, that every phenomenon could be explained in techno-language or by throwing more money at it. Helen genuinely disliked people who were narrow minded.

"I keep my options open," she said mustering a stern voice. "I prefer to remain unprejudiced rather than wincing sceptically, like most people, at unexplained phenomena or the unexplainable. Anyway I don't merely believe for beliefs sake. There's a good deal more substance, more credibility to unexplained supernatural occurrences than what I may say. Why do you think I have become a member of the British Psychic and Occult Society. Want evidence? Why don't you write to them ? Or come with me to have your palm read at Covent Garden. Or how about it, Uncle Stuart, I'm quite willing to lend you my ticket to the London Dungeon."

His matter-of-fact stockbroker face had creased up with cynical amusement and disbelief.

However, now Helen could shrug a shoulder at this in the wake of the College of Music letter, and imagine herself free. In just a matter of days she would be her own person. Her first task was to collect the keys to her new room from the Cello Course tutor for this term. The acceptance letter even contained mention of the Council engineer's report which vouched that her newly renovated room in Spitalfields was structurally safe.

Pocketing the letter, Helen left Uncle Stuart's apartment *en route* to the College of Music, leaving her rucksack and cello on his lounge floor for the last time. The following day the move happened so rapidly that it was difficult to believe in her luck. After scrubbing the walls of her little renovated room, Helen decided to paint them pale peach with matt white window and door frames. After applying the second coat of paint, surveying her labour, Helen noticed a different texture to one area of the wall as though a door had been bricked-in and plastered over. She wondered whether the Council engineer knew about this apparently blocked recess ? When she tapped the brickwork there was a dry, hollow sound.

Her single sash window overlooked a Hawksmoor Church located at the bottom of the street. It was a religious looking building of sturdy white stone. On her first night Helen drew the curtains across this church atmosphere to block out its severe shadows in the alcoves and its columned, steepled silhouette. And fell asleep half-thinking, happily half-dreaming about the simple decorations still to be arranged. Her pastel rug would blend well with the newly painted wall colour combination; she would place pot plants around to add greenery; on the fireplace mantle she would line up her framed family photo's (including pictures of her on-stage music performances). Her cello was leaning in one corner of the little room beneath where she had pinned a poster of Mozart to strategically block that bricked-in part of the wall.

*

"Kenneth, may I have a word ?"
"If you're quick, Helen. I must catch a class."

"I'm sorry to have to ask this..." Helen said, tentative and slightly embarrassed, glancing floorwards while standing in the cluttered communal hallway at the entrance to Kenneth's bedroom. With one hand casually in his pocket, Kenneth was using the other to dig around in a rucksack to check he had packed everything needed for his college class. He looked up to the enquiring Helen: "But did you perhaps discover a stray ten pound note anywhere in the house ?" she asked. "Seems I've mislaid a tenner."

Kenneth continued his rummaging. "You're not accusing me of anything, are you ?"

"No, not at all," Helen said, quite taken aback.

"I hope not. If you've lost money already, I'm sorry to hear that. I know nothing about it." He shook his head emphatically. Of the three students Helen shared this new house with, Kenneth had occupied this Brushfield Street address longer than anyone. Apparently, so she overheard, Kenneth was a veritable computer boffin. Like Uncle Stuart he seemed a matter-of-fact type, super-rational, a person who probably kept to himself.

When her other two housemates were asked the same question, they elicited a similar negative response to finding any mislaid money and they recoiled at Helen's suspicions too. All of them seemed honest. Trustworthy.

It shocked Helen to lose this amount of cash: as a student struggling financially she had always tried to prevent this kind of loss.

Later in the afternoon Kenneth entered her brightly painted room and watched Helen still conducting a search. "Can I help you look ?"

"It's definitely not here. I tell you, my dosh is kept in this jacket pocket and I always hang the jacket here on this side of the cupboard. No holes in the pocket, see..." She unhooked the jacket, held it up and displayed it on her forefinger. She thanked Kenneth for caring.

Subsequently Helen took the extra precaution of closing her bedroom door and locking it when the jacket was hanging up, whilst careful not to arouse suspicion from her housemates. She would hate them to imagine she may be paranoid or for this issue to become a talking point. It even felt embarrassing that Kenneth seemed so interested because the more she got acquainted with him the more she realized that, like Uncle Stuart, he would probably rebut any talk about the occult as nonsense.

Some weeks later, the incident now at the back of Helen's mind, a crisp fifty pound rent-note she had sealed in a plain white envelope in the same jacket pocket, disappeared also. This time it vanished from within her closed bedroom with the door securely bolted. With

127

intense agitation she rounded up her housemates for an emergency meeting.

"Look, I realize that apart from ourselves, no visitors have been here today. But how on earth could fifty pounds simply vanish from my room ?" Helen could no longer disguise her degree of frustration.

"Are you certain it's disappeared ?" asked one.

"Absolutely. I've searched everywhere. I have turned my bedroom upside down again."

The others remained meditative. Silent. Baffled. In the end Kenneth rose and telephoned the Metropolitan Police for her sake. When the police arrived at the Spitalfields house, a man and woman police constable, Helen explained at length the whole story and signed an official statement confirming: 'Loss of private property with suspicion of robbery'.

*

Passing a flowerseller one Saturday morning who had come to recognize her in the neighbourhood, who would tip his hat in greeting, Helen overheard him mention the white stone Hawksmoor Church across the way. The church which each night she closed her curtains to and which faced her bedroom window. Circling the flower buckets to listen in on this conversation, she noticed that in the light of day the shadowy and eery presence of the church had vanished. Today its facade presided over the noisy bustle of East End shoppers and fish and vegetable sellers at the old Spitalfields market.

"Two cauli's for one !" A stallholder shouted as Helen strained to hear the flowerseller's conversation.

"Iceberg lettuce, two for 30 pence."

"Bowl of brussels half price !"

"Fresh swedes at 26p a pound..."

Courteously the flowerseller tipped his hat at seeing Helen, above these sounds of commerce: a loud, cockney-accented shouting of prices, and continued with his involved discussion about the church.

"It's weird you know," he admitted. "Sometimes early mornings when the wind blows along those stone columns there's a kind of human shrieking sound."

"Hah, hah, hah..." a person burst out.

Listening, Helen inhaled the pungent odour of English and continental cheeses, Dutch edam and ripe French camembert, from a nearby stall.

"What's so funny ?" asked the flowerseller.

"You're daft," said another person. "This is 1990. Ghosts you reckon ? You gotta be joking !"

Shaking his head vigorously the flowerseller affected a serious mood. "Now just you wait a minute. I've lived here forty years. I know this neighbourhood like this fag end and it's not the first time."

Helen broke in: "You know I'm sure that church spire emits a yellow glow on some nights."

The flowerseller rotated his calloused hand. "Dunno about a glow, love. Can't say I've ever seen it do that, can't say. But I've heard some eery sounds coming from over there... eh, s'truth, I've heard them human wails something awful. Mind you, it wasn't long ago when they discovered those unburied coffins down in the crypt."

"Unburied coffins !" Helen gasped.

"Aye love, this is Jack-the-Ripper territory. Many years ago he struck just a little way over there."

Helen forgot to enquire from the flowerseller about the price of two bunches of daffodils she had been eyeing. Instead, dazed by this new information, she rapidly left the scene and for hours that night lay awake wondering about the disturbed history of this neighbourhood. And if, possibly, it could have been a poltergeist that had stolen her money. What else could remove money so efficiently from behind her locked door, she wondered. Yes, indeed, who or what else ? But what would a poltergeist want with earthly money ?

On entering the kitchen early one Sunday morning to find a toilet-roll streamered in a strange zigzag across the floor, the rest of the house silent and fast asleep, Helen stood rigid in front of this scene.

"Sweet Lord deliver us," she muttered to herself. "Now it's moved beyond my bedroom !"

The book on 'Paranormal Activity' that she had loaned from the local library advised that she measure atmospheric pressure and air temperature at intervals before and after such events to quantify the effects. She had no such equipment. Instead, Helen tried to calm herself and decided to begin to monitor these things in a personal diary: their occurrences, she felt, were becoming too frequent now to be dismissed. Writing down what had previously happened led to all kinds of new questions being raised in Helen's mind. Recalling the alleged poltergeist events already passed she realized that Kenneth was always present in the house at these times. Was he involved ?

Some few nights later an explosive crash of glass from the kitchen jolted Helen awake. With the house in darkness the time was 1.30 in the morning. She jotted this time in her diary under an arc of torchlight. Glancing out of the window, she shivered inwardly at that creepy yellow glow of the Hawksmoor Church steeple. Or did the glow emanate from a spotlight beam ? There was no time to consider that. At this instant what mattered was to monitor the poltergeist. The responsibility – as yet secret - had fallen squarely on her shoulders. Helen slipped into her gown whilst trying to control the trembling that was her fear and crept stealthily past bicycles parked in the hallway. Peering into the kitchen she saw a figure floating around the dark: it opened the fridge door and in the crack of light...

"Kenneth ! Bloody hell, you gave me a fright."

"Helen," Kenneth whispered. "Did you hear it ?"

"What ?"

"That crash. I came to look."

In their mutual search around the kitchen they discovered a shattered bowl of noodles overturned from the dining table onto the tiled floor. The more Helen contemplated the growing sequence of events listed in her diary, and the more unexplainable these happenings to the extent of resembling the supernatural, the more she felt a necessity to know why her bedroom had only been used for storage by previous occupants of the house. Until now it had never been a bedroom. What about that bricked-in part of the wall ? Behind the poster of Mozart. All these ominous happenings had begun around the time she moved into her little renovated room.

Kenneth smiled. "Maybe that bowl of noodles was positioned badly on the table."

"You mean and suddenly just drop off !" she said.

"What else Helen ?"

In the kitchen dimness and the quiet of early morning, it was then that Helen decided to convey to Kenneth her long thought out impressions of the chain of yet unexplainable events. She couldn't yet tell him she was secretly monitoring the process. That was unnecessary at this stage. But in her exposition she did include, of course, a history of the background of Hawksmoor church crypt and the fact that this was once Jack-the-Ripper territory to test his reaction. Tactfully in the process she slipped in her poltergeist theory. Kenneth was amused. Nothing more. Except he touched her shoulder with tenderness and brushed a finger against her cheek, which she found irritating.

Two months following the disappearance of that first ten-pound note of money, Helen believed that a jigsaw of facts was beginning to fit into place. She realized this on a walk home after visiting the Council offices where a structural engineer had explained that sealed behind her bedroom wall was a Victorian kitchen. Turning into Brushfield street, Helen noticed how all the brand new glass office blocks being built around the revamped Liverpool Street Station were encroaching up the road towards the Hawksmoor church, replacing Victorian and Edwardian terraced houses.

Was the neighbourhood presently being demolished actually haunted ? She waved a greeting to the friendly flowerseller. And back in her little room upstairs whilst practising on the cello, a scratching sound began to emanate from behind the bricked-in panel. Helen wasn't sure whether to continue her playing and not distract the strange noise since this would be her first daytime evidence. She continued to play. Until, with growing apprehension, she botched a chord and stopped Beethoven's Egmont overture. The scratching also ceased. Her panic began to rise. Am I strong enough for this, she wondered ? Tentatively she decided to stand up, leaning the cello against her bed in order to flee and when the scratching started again, in her rising fear Helen silently eased her way out of the half open bedroom door, cello bow still in hand.

*

In the hallway she waited for what seemed minutes while her breathing heaved with the rapid pulsing of her heartbeat. Imagining that behind the bricked-in part of the wall a poltergeist dressed in a Victorian apron and bonnet, dragging a leg-iron, was attempting to escape by scratching a hole through. What would she do when it appeared ? Throw a bowl of noodles back at it ? Pay it more money to go away ? Hold up a wooden crucifix ? Or like some daughter of Boadicea heap faggots upon it and burn it with a bag of gunpowder around its neck !

Helen shuddered at this dilemma. There was something suspicious in her room. It was no laughing matter. Trying to steady her nerves, she leaned up against the passage wall. At this moment only one other person was present in the house, as usual, and that was Kenneth. Can he be trusted, she wondered ? To ease the dryness in her throat she swallowed a few times. But as the scratching noise re-established itself in a muffled way behind the door...

"Kenneth ! Come here quick !" Helen called.

"I'm busy programming my computer," he replied casually, as if she were wasting his time. "If you need me you can come here."

When Helen reached the small alcove preceding his bedroom that was used as his study, she did not enter but placed a hand on the doorframe which quelled her nervous shaking and stood in a high-strung state, watching him at work. The scratching poltergeist was too distant to be heard now. Obviously Kenneth had not been the cause ! Now he could not be implicated. His back to her with shoulders relaxed, sitting at a computer screen, he was oblivious of her arrival or her anxious state of mind. She knocked feebly on the open door.

"Wait a minute..." he said.

Words which tapered off into an echoing in her skull: a kind of spinning sensation while still holding onto the doorframe facing him. Except that a new feeling was overcoming her in which she was beginning to float and could see herself in her mind's eye. Distant, somewhere earthwards, she visualised herself clutching the door support - the cello bow held in her free hand. From high up the bow dropped to the floor. Kenneth turned around, his movements too had begun to spin in her mind as his voice echoed:

"Goodness grief, Helen. Your face is white !"

Unable to prevent her legs from crumpling into a body collapse, the carpet rushing upwards, she held out a hand to avoid falling onto the cello bow. Then there was a soft blackness. Silence. Deep and heavy. Followed by a distant, repeated calling out of her name and a slapping of her cheek. She was being raised yet felt completely limp, unable to move, while someone lifted and carried her. Eventually the head spinning stopped.

"What happened ?" she groaned as Kenneth peered anxiously over her.

"You fainted, Helen. Are you all right ?"

He offered a glass of sugar water to her. With care he placed a hand on her forehead to feel the temperature. Lifting her throbbing head, she sipped at the liquid sweetness, feeling then a headache in moving her neck. She stared upwards to the ceiling. Closed her eyes. It took some minutes before she realized that she was back in her little bedroom.

"Get me out of here !" Helen lashed out, sitting up and knocking the glass of sugar water from Kenneth's hand. It splattered onto the floor. She pushed him off the bed to his feet while she herself swivelled around... until that headache caused a cringe of pain. It braced her like a spasm, paralysing her in a heavy-laden head vice. She pressed her temples. Then delicately she swivelled back into a supine position to lay her head back on the pillow. When Kenneth again sat down beside her, causing the bed to move ever slightly, she frowned in discomfort. Helen's face remained a pallid colour. Her mouth was dry, her tongue felt furry and swollen as if she had been yelling out loud during the faint. Briefly she shut her eyes, exhausted, then was surprised to look up at him as he planted a kiss on her nose.

"Sounds were coming from behind that wall," she murmured.

Kenneth gave a puzzled expression.

In a subdued way, whilst moving her finger in a circular massage over her right temple, she continued: "It sounded like someone trying to scratch their way out. That's why I called out to you."

"That's why you fainted ?" he said in disbelief.

"There must be a poltergeist behind that wall."

"Ah, you're not harping on about that again." Drawing in his breath, Kenneth shook his head with heavy judgement. But the seriousness on her face remained no matter the added headache and pain in her eyes. "Look Helen, you've got to try to get beyond all these emotional reactions. I've lived in this neighbourhood much longer than you and I've heard people around here concoct the weirdest stories, myths and superstitions."

She eyed him with cynicism. "Why would anyone concoct a poltergeist ?"

"Why... Because we're in Spitalfields. Because the locals around here claim all kinds of sightings. Conjur up all kinds of visions: because this place has a long, dark history attached to it."

"All the more reason."

"Don't be ridiculous. We're living in 1990. In my four years here I haven't met anyone whose story hasn't panned out to be some bizarre fabrication of their mind."

"Well I'm sorry but in this instance you've got it very wrong," Helen's mood was insistent as she continued the circular massage of her temples. "I agree that circumstantial evidence is one thing. But it's entirely another matter..." Her eyes widened. She grabbed at Kenneth's leg.

From behind the cupboard a scratching sound had resumed. She felt the muscles in Kenneth's leg go taut as she pulled her own knees to her chest defensively in foetal position. A pounding began again inside her head as she watched Kenneth's face go gaunt even while he tried to retain his composure. The cupboard between them and the door meant that they were both trapped in her room.

"For God's sake calm yourself, Helen."

She whimpered. Kenneth decided to arm himself with her spare cello bow. For once he looked nervous. Apprehensive. And vulnerable with this musical weapon. Hesitantly he approached her jacket hanging on the cupboard peg while the dry scratching sound continued. With the cello bow outstretched at the ready, Kenneth resembled the contour of a strange medieval swordsman:

he placed his boot under the foot of the cupboard, hooked it and pulled.

It is here that the rest of the story is far from clear. Kenneth at first claimed categorically that he saw a black rat leap out. Or something definitely alive (he later adjusted his certainty for opinion when they had a house discussion about it) which had careered across the floor, disappearing behind a pot plant where a displaced brick in the bricked-in recess left a narrow breach to the other side. It was true that, on later inspection behind the pot plant, there was indeed a hole in the wall. Helen remembered a concrete block which workmen had removed when clearing her room which must have sealed this hole. But she herself did not see the alleged rat. Lying on the bed, one eye obscured by a pillow, she had observed a shadowy movement which, unlike a rodent, seemed to scamper but then evaporate in a puff from her jacket.

"Well there's your poltergeist," Kenneth said with authority, although still holding his heart. "There's the culprit: a mother rodent looking for food and bits of nesting paper for its young. All your pound notes must be behind the wall in its nest !"

"Are you certain. Did you see its tail ?"

At first Kenneth looked at her blankly. Straight off he could not say undoubtedly, that yes he had seen a tail. He seemed more intent on reassuring her. Allaying her fears. So he remained firmly attached to this easier rodent conviction as if his mind refused any darker alternatives. It was a jumble of assurances that penetrated the fog of her headache and before she knew it, Kenneth was kissing her on the mouth. She was caught off guard. Partly relieved to have any kind of answer. And partly surprised and subdued by how responsive she became to his kiss. As suddenly he left the room to retrieve that old concrete block in order to replace it and seal the hole in the wall.

When he was gone, Helen lay alone, less convinced of this answer than Kenneth had been. A rat can't explain it all, she knew. Being by herself again sparked her independence of thought. It didn't seem to explain those other phenomena, those eery shrieks from Hawksmoor church crypt or other sightings in Spitalfields. Ought she to raise this poltergeist issue at the next meeting of the British Psychic and Occult Society ?

She sat up. Wouldn't it be nice to think that Kenneth was on her side but she knew he was too much the sceptic. The tingle of that delicious kiss could still be felt as a taste in her mouth. If he wasn't with her in this poltergeist problem, the task of monitoring would once again have to fall squarely onto her shoulders, conducted in secret, noting down dates and times of any new disturbances. So be it, she thought, straightening up. The hole in the wall would be sealed up properly. But how would it affect the poltergeist ? She leaned over to reach her diary on the bedside table. Opened it. And read the foreword which she had written many weeks ago in her handwriting and which she absolutely stood by to this day:

IN THE EVENT OF MY UNEXPLAINED
DISAPPEARANCE,
READ THIS DIARY.

142

MEMBERS ENCLOSURE AT LORD'S
(1991 Benson & Hedges Cup Final)

Here where the cricket heartbeat is clothed
in emblems, ties, double-breasted blazers;
we're marshalled into the Warner Stand with
an aplomb that's moustached and official.

We sit, blink at this famous green oval
that's the world stamping ground of wickets;
seated behind ad's: HAMLET CIGARS, NATWEST
BRITANNIC ASSURANCE, COTTON OXFORD, TEXACO.

Muttered talk of England versus West Indies
in the smell of hot salt-beef sandwiches;
the scoreboard clears to an announcement:
"Lancashire win the toss and will field".

Chink of champagne glasses, and peanuts
are offered by a man in starched kipper tie;
"Ah, Curtis bowled by De Freitas for four !"
explodes the crowd in bullroar thousands.

Then another batsman taps bat on crease
head over shoulder at the attacking bowler;
with his heartbeat padded, helmeted too
against the puff of a speeding trajectory.

"I've told you how to play ball, Willie..."
said an anxious Mrs Martha Grace years ago;
whose son now stands 'far beyond rivalry'
for turning his wooden bat into a roll-call

of Bradman, Ranji, of Richards and Gooch,
whereupon this sacrosanct turf at Lord's
they deflect, hit, and confound opponents
in this atmosphere that is old England.

BY THE VEGETABLE PATCH

The strange man moved next door sometime in May. Indeed, yes, I cannot deny that from the start he seemed to me an unusual man, perhaps I ought even to call him in retrospect a strange hero, for if I were truthful to myself that is what he has come to represent now. He and his friends - four of them - moved next door towards the end of the month, I believe it was, when in north London the tepid spring sunshine is making way for that more glorious and intense heat of the English summer.

Though it was some weeks before this time that I met the woman whom he came with and who was to be the new South African owner of this house.

One day there was a brisk knock at my door and a woman in her mid-thirties, straight-talking and very capable, powerful in her bearing, introduced herself. She said in a friendly way that she was one of the two South African's moving in, who were to be my next door neighbours. There would be two more women accompanying her and the single man, and I recognised some time later that these other three were younger than her: around their late twenties. My visitor that day and her female colleague had managed to raise enough capital and a hefty bank loan to buy the house in order to start a day-care nursery.

"Of course, we will be having renovations," she told me excitedly. It was then that I detected the foreign voice. I asked her about the strong South African accent. And was quite astonished - equally intrigued - to hear her admit that her father had spent 22 years as a political prisoner in a Pretoria jail. Telling me this with a definite pride in her tone of voice and stature. Yes, she confirmed, born in Cape Town in South Africa as was her mother and brother. But this fatherless threesome had fled the country in fear when she was only eight years old at the time her father was imprisoned. Yet after nearly thirty years living in England her accent was still prominent. Then she mentioned the strange young man whom she said had arrived freshly fled from the ongoing apartheid politics of that embattled country and who was to be the only male occupier of this large five bedroom house next door.

The first time I glimpsed these four new neighbours together was some weeks after the builders and renovators had begun their work. They had scaffolded the place, and I was becoming irritated by the incessant noise of drills, hammers, the groan of a tiller biting hard into garden soil. On the date she had given me the three women duly arrived by car with a removals van trailing them. Behind my net curtains I watched anonymously as they set about co-ordinating the activities of a team of removal men: pointing this way and that at boxes that were streaming into the house.

Then one of them departed in an estate car: I recognised her as the older woman who came to visit me, and shortly she returned with a man sitting in the passenger seat. Obviously he was the fourth member of their group to be moving in. Greeted happily by the other women - clearly they were pleased to see him - one seemed to joke, from my angle of vision I could see her humorous gestures, about the scant luggage that he was carrying: just a single suitcase in one hand and a portable typewriter in the other, which indeed did contrast with that pantechnicon parked outside so heavily-laden with their boxes. I was struck immediately by the strange way in which this young man carried himself. As they all entered their new home.

Days passed. When next the young man reappeared I was involved with freelance journalistic activities in my study. This time he happened to appear in the back garden. Over my desk, through the sash window, I had an unobstructed view across the low wooden fence that separates our two properties. The elder of the three women (who I now know by first-name to be Ruth) was explaining something that appeared important to him as they both watched workmen laying turf over the recently tilled, fertilized backyard soil.

It seemed as though the renovations were progressing according to plan. By exterior appearance of the house, that is, which was as much obviously as I could make out. Windows were now double-glazed, the roof had been re-tiled, and apart from an entirely revamped garden (the latest major undertaking) I gathered from the internal noises coming through my wall that a considerable upheaval was taking place inside.

Ruth, however, and the young man whose strangely forlorn gait has begun to fascinate me, had fixed their attention on the new lawn being unrolled and fitted into place like a jigsaw. While unbeknown to them I watched with an unobtrusive eye from the darkened recess of my study.

Half the garden at the bottom farthest end was now smoothed down and a patchwork of green lawn. This part looked complete. Whilst the workmen continued their job of unraveling turf in places that I could not see. Ruth followed the young South African man along a path of paving stones that dissected this lower area of garden. Talking to him as she pointed towards a sector of grass. He nodded in agreement the place she was pointing to, and began to pace out a precise rectangle of lawn the size of which became a matter of discussion amongst themselves (how many paces length and width it should be). A consensus of opinion between the two of them led Ruth to walk beyond my angle of vision but she was back briskly with a workman in tow.

And I was surprised by what followed. She gave the workman instructions to peel up the allotted rectangle of newly-laid lawn which they had just paced out. Purposefully asking the workman, with set movements of her hands, to demarcate the boundary of this strange rectangle of soil with split logs.

*

It's the way that young man carries himself, I guess, which must have prompted it, and my ever curious journalistic mind that prompted me to turn to the section on South African politics in the local Haringey library. It was the first time ever that an opportunity like this had arisen for me to observe a political exile freshly fled from that apartheid country where he had opposed the infamous racist white government.

Admittedly I have met many white South African exiles here in London - many having just salvaged their lives and often the core of their sanity from the experience of escaping the system of racial laws that so restricts people's lives there. Some such exiles I have met are still highly committed to their cause of non-racialism. And would dearly love to go back when the apartheid government is replaced. While other exiles I have met seem to come here merely to build upon their affluence and try to maintain a racial superiority to which they have become accustomed in apartheid South Africa.

But I have been wondering if there may be a single thing that may bind all these South African exiles ? Those in England seeking freedom. And those prejudiced 'whites' who are here to escape the 'black' man. Maybe there is a common denominator they all share? Which is one thing I hope to witness in this new male neighbour whom Her Majesty's Government has classified *Political Refugee from South Africa awaiting Asylum.* And that is the private emotional world he, and I am told other South African exiles face each day: away from a country both brutal and beautiful. That must indeed be difficult to come to terms with. Yes, as I have gathered from people in the know, it is a country quite impossible to forget.

Now how can anyone imagine that I myself am imposing my viewpoint on the situation or spying ? I am merely a neighbour who, by default, is bound to glimpse small fragments of the private emotional world of those living next door. So having taken this as my mandate to proceed, I have gathered on my desk a pile of relevant library books and other research material. Over the past few days I've pored over these as systematically as journalists are trained to do: kneading out the South African facts from fancy, the relevant from irrelevant. Not unlike a surgeon who makes his incision in the body and knows that there is much prodding, cleaning away, delving to be done before the particular site of one's interest is exposed.

My search through these texts on South Africa has been focused beyond just the political statements of fact about the policies of that country. Of a place infamous for its racism, where a white skin was deemed superior and right - WHERE WHITE BECAME UNBRIDLED RESTRICTIONS AND MIGHT - and for forty years the black majority in that country have legally been denied the most basic democratic rights by a system of immoral laws and separate racial development called apartheid (which is now collapsing). That is not specialist knowledge. Of this, in 1990, the whole world is aware and apartheid branded: 'a crime against humanity'.

Like a surgeon I have been delving for something much more specific to pin the tail onto the donkey, as the saying goes. After all my neighbour, the strange young man, is white. Yet carries himself with such a body of internal scarring: in the way he walks, in the frown on his face, in his subtle gestures and expressions seen even from the distance of my window that I am searching for something that seems only to have been hedged around in these South African novels, research papers, political manifesto's on my desk.

A search which for me seems to be taking on an imperative and fascination. Which raises the question: what happens to the human soul - to its values of altruism, sharing, togetherness - when for more than a generation people are forced to deny those very essences of a shared humanity ? And how deeply felt are these essences involving a young white South African like this ? Because when you deny almost a whole society its basic humanity of freedom, surely by that denial process alone, you are denying the 'white' part of that society its humanity too.

By my estimation and Ruth's second informative yet brief conversation with me the other day, it seems that the young man must have been born around the time of the 1960 State of Emergency in South Africa, and he left his country during its fifth nationwide State of Emergency. That in itself speaks volumes. That such inhuman and uprooting events should mark the boundaries of anyone's young life is sad. But again, this is merely dappling in political statistics which does not reflect the way a person deals with, copes with, confronts these life experiences. So many books on my desk tell of assassinations and brutal torture of both black and white South Africans opposed to living under apartheid. Endless bannings and censorship and the making of exiles. The daily apartheid indoctrination of separate racial development. Separate lives. Impoverishing the soul. How human rights of togetherness are criminalized, bluntened and ridiculed.

That these facts, like the heart and lungs and liver, help the surgeon to find his way around the body. And any weakness or failure in these organs to function normally will point to a reason why the whole body may become diseased. But what is more frightening to me in this case of my neighbour is that warping of the human soul: scarring it internally where the surgeon cannot get to the scars, that is another matter entirely.

So I have turned back to my observation of him. I have put the South African library books away. Though I am still acting, however, as the surgeon who now knows a little better the anatomy of the problem at hand: who can see the outward symptoms more clearly albeit from a distance, yet is afraid that the disease may have spread too widely for any simple incisions. Who must instead wait, watch, monitor the patient's progress for signs of a natural healing process. Where so much malignancy remains in the soul: to be self or socially exorcized. If got rid of at all.

*

It appears that that rectangle of upturned lawn with its boundary demarcated by split logs has been chosen by the young man to be a vegetable patch. At the earliest time he set about transforming this little territory of earth

154

given to him by Ruth. Picking at each individual weed and unwanted stone and imperfection like a hen carefully choosing its nest; determining a place that feels comfortable and protected enough in which to lay its eggs. At first it seemed to me absurd that with all the noise and movement going on within the house, I could hear it clearly through my wall, all the others were rearranging furniture and settling in, that here he was alone spending so much time crouched down and preparing this little vegetable patch as if his life depended on it. It seemed so unnecessary, so premature and out of context under the circumstances. Until I began to realize what was happening...

It struck me one day when Ruth took him a cup of tea. By now he had furrowed the patch into a series of narrow parallel trenches running perpendicular to the fence. With a rake he was busy breaking up the clods into fine soil, raking it into ridges between the gulleys, and he had already planted a row of herbs on the ridge furthest away. Raking with a slowness as if pulling some invisible weight – like pulling a psychological weight along with him. She approached him that day with an equal reticence, a strange hesitancy as though not wanting to disturb. Though there was no pity nor sentimentality in her attitude. Instead I could sense she knew that he must just be left alone here: to stand and ever slowly work the patch. So her conversation was minimal. Even though all he was doing was raking.

And I could see etched on her face when she walked back in my direction (that perhaps she didn't show him) - a kind of hurt that was exactly his, a sudden frown of caring and acceptance with her eyes lowered in solidarity - that was so different to the self-assuredness which she had revealed in her neighbourly visits to me.

That I've given up my ambitions playing the 'surgeon'. I have thrown away those childish problem-solving journalistic illusions in embarrassment. Seeing Ruth interacting with him makes me realize how superbly inadequate and cack-handed this circumstance makes me. Just as well, for his sake, that I'm hidden from view because it is plain that the surgeon is already out there ! It makes me kick myself. Smile at my folly. Shake my head in self-correction. How the obvious jumps out at you sometimes. Now I will have to go back to being simply the shadowy observer. Which in turn places a new light onto Ruth, makes me consider her with renewed interest.

Although one sunset I did actually meet him briefly. By accident it was, following an afternoon of intense London sunshine – an unusually sweltering heat which drove even the grey squirrels and the European starlings back into the woodlands nearby. He had erected a green tarpaulin of plastic fixed onto dowel sticks over the patch which had successfully thrown the vegetables into shade during the hottest time of the day. There was talk over the radio of water restrictions: a possible hose-pipe ban from this weekend onwards, but someone as determined as him, I knew, would keep the vegetable patch going even if it came down to a watering can. I could even picture him bringing out a glass of water or using an eye-dropper if it came to that.

This heat had frazzled my own flowerbeds; one was against the fence adjoining his piece of land. It gave me an opportunity to peek over and examine his handiwork at close-quarters. His tomatoes had climbed right up the netting afixed to the fence and were laden with fat unripe fruit. The broad-beans: the focus of so much of his attention which had to be transplanted and resprouted and urged on due to some bug infestation, were now knee-high and healthy. There were two fluffy rows of carrot tops. Onions, lettuce, half a dozen red cabbages coming on.

His sudden appearance startled me. Unexpectedly he walked out of the house into the garden. I quickly turned to watering my flowerbed, to minding my own business, but of course after such long and distant observations as I had made, I was nervous and excited at this final closeness. The light was unfortunately fading behind him: casting a human silhouette bent in places with intense emotion. His silhouette straightened up, its shoulders tensed at seeing me in close proximity to the vegetable patch but then relaxed (as much as the way he carries himself can relax) realizing that I was simply a neighbour watering on the other side of the fence. I was able in this circumscribed light to nod to him in a friendly neighbourly acknowledgement and in return received an innocuous reply that afterwards, only some time afterwards, shook me to the core.

I suppose I wasn't expecting eyes like that. Though after all my hours of observing him I should really have been more prepared. Not that his glance, piercing as it was, was aimed at me in any way. Particularly since he had hardly even been distracted by me. His real attention seemed instead quite magnetised to the vegetable patch. In no time he had bent down, picked up a sample of the days dried earth, breathed it in rubbing thumb and forefinger together and smelling, inhaling. Then he disappeared under the green plastic tarpaulin.

How can I describe it accurately ? Without appearing to read into it too much or distort, by some unwarranted interpretation, that look I saw in his eyes.

They were like eyes of a ghost. Windows on the soul. Eyes that for too long have been denied that essence of a shared humanity, that have had to put up with so much wrenching apart. It was there and then that I realized undeniably that there can be nothing romantic about the realities of apartheid South Africa. And neither can there be anything romantic about his choice of political asylum. Or indeed those emotions swimming in such young green eyes: coloured as green and leafy as the vegetable patch. Perhaps that is what shocked me. The automatic question: how can such depth of disturbance of the soul ever be understood ?

Yet his expression did not arouse pity. Above all else and foremost, there was a curious touch of dignity. I imagine because of his realization of HOW MUCH HE LACKED ! Dignity in that the truth of apartheid, however hurtful, was in himself being faced at last in this way. Faced as a compassionate adult. As it reflected in his mode of walking. In all these ways I imagine he was shouting silently from those depths: we just cannot forget what has happened ! Nor gloss over or pretend any longer, on whatever side, that we are unrepentant, every colour of us, in allowing what has happened ! Or that by some political maneuver or change of power we can suddenly put it all behind us. That would be a greater lie ! And then he looked away.

It is a month since that day. His broad beans are heavy with pods and one row of carrots have matured nicely and been harvested. A change has also come about now in the amount of time Ruth spends at the vegetable patch, as though he were slowly handing it over to her as a living present. The end perhaps of what I now recognize as his self-induced therapy of needing so badly to create alone with his own hands a pocket of life: seed it, grow it, reap it, to believe in and see the power that life has to regenerate itself. Even if only from this small rectangle of soil.

And in his more frequent absences from the garden I hear these days the sound of a typewriter through the wall which separates our two houses. While at the vegetable patch I can sometimes watch his and Ruth's strange soulful tenderness... a *pas de deux* between two white and exiled doves from South Africa.

AS SPRING TEETERS

In the shafted Westminster light,
gaunt light through grey
beams on down
past Cleopatra's Needle,
to where rapeseed
yellows beside young wheat
and lambs.

The barged Thames is still cold
in its undertow,
St. Pauls' sky
pastelled into dawn
is flecked
this morning with sleet.

Oxford Street fashions itself,
softdrink sales rise
in St. James' Park,
as tissue-white
and mauves
drop in a suburban
snowfall of blossoms.

A Buckingham Palace squirrel sunning,

is slow to tail-sweep

its alarm,

beneath warm dovesong

and branch to branch

chases.

In Coldfall Wood

grass-shoots

pierce

through the leaflitter,

the mossy starkness

of treetrunks

is spear-tipped with buds.

While on a Finchley pavement

I walk,

this confetti

of petals spiralling,

as spring teeters,

so London endures as London !

ACKNOWLEDGEMENTS

Acknowledgements are due to the Editors of the following anthologies in which the poems in this volume were first published: CAMDEN VOICES (Summer 1991, London); VERTICAL IMAGES No. 6 (1991, London); KITES No. 15 (1992, London); THE FROGMORE PAPERS No. 35 (1992, Kent), No. 36/37 with North American Supplement (1992, Kent); PARNASSUS OF WORLD POETS (1994, Madras, India).

ABOUT THE AUTHOR

Brandon Broll is a distinguished poet listed in the *International Who's Who in Poetry and Poets' Encyclopaedia*. Author of the bestselling science book *Microcosmos*, he lives in London and is married with two sons.

Printed in Great Britain
by Amazon